## "I know one method to shut you up..."

Sam made a sound of exasperation before grabbing Reese's upper arms and roughly pulling her to him. He hesitated, as if giving her a chance to ward him off, and when she ignored it, he lowered his head and claimed her mouth.

She slid her arms around his neck and kissed him back, her tongue dueling with his, the sudden yearning for his touch burning deep in her belly. Her breasts ached with it, and the temptation to draw him back to the small room and strip him bare fueled an enthusiasm that caught her off guard.

He released her arms, and she briefly thought he might push her away, but he caught her at the waist and then one hand slid around to the small of her back, urging her closer. She sighed into his mouth, and he brought her closer still, until their bodies touched and her breasts crushed against his muscled chest.

"Had enough?" he asked hoarsely.

"Not nearly," she replied, a smile dancing across her lips.

Dear Reader,

Hard to believe that it's been fifteen years since I sold my first book. I'd been reading romance novels long before that, and through two career changes I knew that I wanted to write for Harlequin Books. One day, I bit the bullet and sat at a typewriter. When I finally submitted that first book, I was flat-out rejected. Fortunately I didn't give up, and Harlequin, bless them, didn't give up on me.

I've had a lot of good editors at Harlequin, wonderful women who have rarely said no. It's been their "let's see how we can do this" attitude that has kept me a loyal writer and reader. This book is an excellent example. I've wanted to write a time travel for quite a while now, and although at the time I proposed the idea, Harlequin Blaze wasn't doing paranormals yet, my editor, Kathryn, promptly said, "Maybe—what did you have in mind?" Gotta love the attitude.

Well, you're about to read my first time travel. The research was fun, as was the challenge of writing a character with modern sensibilities facing nineteenth-century mores, and of course, vice versa. I hope you enjoy this story; it's definitely on my short list of favorites to have written.

All my best,

Debbi Rawlins

# Once an Outlaw

## DEBBI RAWLINS

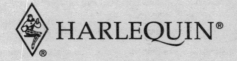

TORONTO • NEW YORK • LONDON
AMSTERDAM • PARIS • SYDNEY • HAMBURG
STOCKHOLM • ATHENS • TOKYO • MILAN • MADRID
PRAGUE • WARSAW • BUDAPEST • AUCKLAND

Recycling programs
for this product may
not exist in your area.

ISBN-13: 978-0-373-79459-1
ISBN-10:    0-373-79459-2

ONCE AN OUTLAW

www.eHarlequin.com

**Printed in U.S.A.**

## ABOUT THE AUTHOR

Debbi Rawlins lives in central Utah, out in the country, surrounded by woods and deer and wild turkeys. It's quite a change for a city girl, who didn't even know where the state of Utah was until four years ago. Of course, unfamiliarity never stopped her. Between her junior and senior years of college she spontaneously left home in Hawaii, and bummed around Europe for five weeks by herself. And much to her parents' delight, returned home with only a quarter in her wallet.

## Books by Debbi Rawlins

Don't miss any of our special offers. Write to us at the following address for information on our newest releases.

Harlequin Reader Service
U.S.: 3010 Walden Ave., P.O. Box 1325, Buffalo, NY 14269
Canadian: P.O. Box 609, Fort Erie, Ont. L2A 5X3

## Dedication

This book is for my mother, Betty, who'd always wanted me to write an historical. And for my husband, Karl, who'd taught me to love history. I miss you both more than I can say.

## Acknowledgment

In 1874 George Armstrong Custer's announcement that gold had been discovered at French Creek triggered the Black Hills Gold Rush and the rise of Deadwood. The town sprang up quickly, reaching a population of over 5,000 in an alarming amount of time, and attracting a slew of businesses from saloons to brothels to dry goods stores. Buildings were hastily erected and sometimes even tents were used by vendors, as well as attorneys plying their trade, but for the purposes of this book, I've focused on a much more scaled-down version of the camp. Also during this period, you will note that some of the newer inventions enjoyed back East were not yet available to the citizens of Deadwood.

# 1

SHE WAS LATE. All because she'd forgotten the necklace and had to go back. Reese Winslow parked her red Beamer convertible illegally, jumped out and raced through the studio doors.

A panicked-looking young woman with blond, spiky bangs, and wearing headphones, jogged toward her. "Dr. Winslow?"

Fingering the smooth jade pendant that hung around her neck, Reese nodded. It was a talisman more than a piece of jewelry, and she hated doing anything important without it.

The woman's relieved expression flirted with annoyance. "Seven minutes to airtime. Will you be ready?"

"I will." Reese pointed to the hall on the left. "This way to makeup, right?"

"Yep. Karla's waiting, but you gotta hurry."

Reese was tempted to pull off her four-inch high heels, but then she'd risk ruining her new hose. When she entered the dressing room, Karla already had a makeup brush in her hand.

"You don't look too bad." The redhead squinted at Reese over gold reading glasses. "I'll have you ready in no time."

"I've got about five minutes." Reese sat in the black leather chair facing the mirror.

Shaking her head, Karla threw a cape over the front of Reese's dress. "Your mother used to always be late, too."

"Oh, please, this is the first time I've been late." She was nothing like her mother, but she didn't want to go there. "I'll bet you a hot fudge sundae I'll be in my seat on time."

Karla snorted and gestured to her curvy right hip. "Do I look like I need a sundae?"

"Don't worry about it. You're losing the bet. Not that I need a sundae, either."

"Oh, brother." The woman shook her head but concentrated on working her magic. "Believe it or not, when I was your age I was a size four, too."

"The camera makes me look like a size twelve," Reese muttered, studying her reflection. "I should've worn my navy blue suit. This green dress makes me look washed out."

Karla exchanged the makeup brush she'd been using to apply blush for a smaller one, while eyeing Reese critically. "No, it brings out the green in your eyes." She went to work on touching up Reese's eye shadow. "Don't worry, honey, the camera loves you."

It was her nerves talking, Reese decided. Which was crazy. She'd been around movie sets her whole life. Before her parents had divorced, and twice as much after. No matter which one she and her sister, Ellie, had been shuttled to, either their mother or father invariably were starring in a movie.

She'd be okay once the camera rolled. Oddly, the last two times she'd been invited to join a panel of physicians, she'd immediately calmed down as soon as the on-the-air signal came. Needing to focus on the questions put before them had rid her of anxiety. Especially since the rest of the panelists were a collection of esteemed doctors a good two decades her senior.

Reese glanced at the large round wall clock. Too bad she

didn't have a tenth of her mother's composure. Or her father's enviable charisma. Brad and Linea Winslow had been Hollywood royalty, the power couple of the seventies and eighties. Even now, close to sixty, they each enjoyed considerable success.

If Reese had wanted a career in show business, the doors would've swung wide open. But from the time she was ten, she wanted to be a doctor. And nothing had swayed her off the path. She'd been blessed with excellent tutors who accompanied her to her parents' sets. Blessed, too, with a scientific mind that had allowed her entrance into one of the best medical schools in the country. Before she'd completed her residency, she'd been invited to join the staff of a prestigious East Coast hospital. Everyone thought she had it made. In many ways she did have everything. At least to the naked eye.

The blonde briefly poked her head into the dressing room. "Two minutes, Dr. Winslow."

Reese breathed in deeply, counting to ten before she exhaled. She wished Ellie could've made it tonight. Her sister was the one constant in her life. The only person who understood her, who'd been by her side through their parents' messy, public divorce, through the holidays spent with their nanny, through the broken promises. Yet even Ellie didn't totally comprehend the depth of Reese's loneliness. How could she possibly complain, when her privileged life had extended into adulthood?

Oh, Ellie had had her successes, too. Including a fabulous modeling career, which she'd chosen to leave. But after that she'd seemed lost, unsure of what she wanted in life. Reese had never faltered from the golden path. She'd inherited her mother's fair looks, only twice suffered the indignation of receiving a grade below an A, and had enjoyed a short list of so-called perfect boyfriends.

Even the recent "celebrity doctor" moniker had come easy, largely due to her family name. She didn't delude herself about that point. But her education, ambition and looks sealed the deal. So how could anything be missing in her life?

Karla unsnapped and pulled off the black cape. "Better get out there, or they'll send in the dogs."

Reese smiled at the seasoned older woman, whom she'd gotten to know a little during the past few months, since she'd been making the health panel circuit. The makeup artist had crossed paths with Reese's mother over the years, and sadly, seemed to know more about Linea Winslow than Reese did. She enjoyed the stories about her parents, though, and after she got to her feet, gave the woman an impulsive hug.

Karla blinked, clearly surprised at the gesture. Her expression softened. "You're gonna do great, honey."

Unnerved by her own uncharacteristic display of affection, Reese pulled back her shoulders and nodded brusquely before heading out of the room. She didn't know what was wrong. Why the sudden melancholy. Maybe it was simply the dreaded chore that lay ahead for her and Ellie tomorrow. One they had put off for too long. Packing up Grandma Lily's house in South Dakota.

A year had already passed since her funeral and the reading of the will that left all of her possessions to Reese and Ellie, including the grand old house that had been in the Winslow family for over a hundred thirty years. Even when they were children the three-story house had seemed ancient, with its creaking doors and noisy hardwood floors.

With Grandma Lily having been moved to a retirement community nine years ago, Reese hadn't been back to the home since she was twenty. She didn't look forward to returning and not seeing Grandma Lily sitting on the wraparound porch, rocking in her favorite faded, rust-colored chair. It was going to be strange and depressing, but the Realtor had called three times now with the same interested buyer, and it was foolish to allow the place to rot away.

With Ellie's upcoming photography show and Reese about to start her position at the hospital, the timing to clear out the old place would never be better than right now.

"Ready, Dr. Winslow?" A short, stocky young man with thinning brown hair gestured her toward the stage, where the rest of the panel members were already seated. Three men and one other woman with a staggering combined knowledge that should've humbled Reese.

And it did. To some extent. But she was no slouch, either. Straightening, she touched the jade that had been in the Winslow family for eons, smiled at the assistant and then took her place on stage.

REESE SLOWED the rental car, virtually stopping in shock before turning into the overgrown driveway.

Ellie gasped. "Oh, my God. I can't believe this mess. Maybe we should park on the street. The car is likely to get scratched."

"You're right." Reese slowly reversed, narrowly missing the wooden mailbox that sagged to the side. Guilt tugged at her heart. Where beautiful yellow and pink roses once followed the curve of the porch, weeds choked the life out of anything in their path. "I guess we shouldn't be too surprised."

"I am. The Realtor swore he'd keep the place maintained. We've sent him four checks."

Reese stopped the car just short of the brick sidewalk that led through the gate to the porch steps. "True. I can't believe he has a buyer."

"Maybe that's why he's let everything get run-down. Mr. Kent told me the man wants to tear the place down and build a bed-and-breakfast." Ellie shook her dark head as she reached for the handle and opened her door. "Still, this is awful."

Reese pulled the key from the ignition and stared at her sister. "He wants to tear it down?"

Ellie shrugged. "I'm pretty sure that's what Mr. Kent said. I was meeting with a client when he called."

"That's crazy."

Ellie frowned, her annoyance plain, and totally understandable. She'd received little help from Reese with the matter. "Can you imagine how much it would cost to restore just the house? Not to mention the garage and carriage house."

Reese didn't say anything. She had no right. It wasn't as if she was willing to step in and do anything with the old place. Her life was far removed from the Black Hills of South Dakota. In fact, not until she'd pulled up to the rickety, once-white picket fence did she feel the sentimental pull of the three summers she and Ellie had spent here in Deadwood.

No doubt there would've been many more summers, too, if Grandma Lily hadn't started with the strange haunted house stories that scared the living daylights out of two different nannies.

Both sisters got out of the car, and Ellie, reaching the gate first, gingerly lifted the metal catch. The peeling paint wasn't so bad, but the rotting wood was more than an eyesore, rendering the gate pretty useless. One of the slats fell off when she tugged a little too hard.

"Wow. This is scary. I hope the floorboards inside are okay," Reese said, her gaze going to the blue front door, which, oddly, looked freshly painted.

"Mr. Kent wouldn't have been able to show the house if it was unsafe."

"You'd think."

"Yeah." Ellie's laugh was nervous. "Maybe we should've had someone else come pack up the house."

Reese glared at her. "Gee, that sounds familiar."

"I know. I know. That's what you wanted to do from the beginning. Too impersonal. Grandma deserved more than that."

Reese looked away. She refused to feel guilty about being rational. Her time was at a premium. Ellie, much more a free spirit, didn't always understand that.

"Anyway, we would've hated not knowing what was in those old trunks in the attic."

Sighing, Reese followed her up the front steps, which were surprisingly sturdy. "You're right. Besides, do you know how long it's been since we've gotten together? No parents. No photographers. No deadlines. Just us."

"Not my fault."

Reese made a face. "I know."

Ellie chuckled and nudged her with her shoulder. "I'm glad we're here, too."

Reese had the key and inserted it in the lock. At first it stuck, but after some wiggling, she opened the door, immediately greeted by the faint lingering scent of their grandmother's lavender and a collage of childhood memories. For a moment she was ten again, giddy with the memory of glorious months running barefoot and gorging herself with homemade chocolate chip cookies until she thought she'd be sick.

She slanted her sister a mischievous smile. "Race you to the back door."

Sensible Ellie's eyes widened. "But the floorboards—"

"You are so going to lose." Laughing, Reese lurched over the threshold and into the dusty abyss.

REESE AWOKE the next morning in her old room, feeling more refreshed than she had in weeks. A little dusting, and fresh linens on the Victorian-style rosewood double bed, had made the place more comfy than the motel rooms they had reserved, so they'd canceled their reservations, grabbed dinner in town, picked up a few groceries and crashed early.

"About time you got up." Already dressed in jeans and a god-awful pink T-shirt, Ellie stood at the bottom of the stairs. "Coffee is ready."

"I smell it. Bless you." In her favourite sweats, Reese yawned, and carefully walked down the stairs. "You better not have gone to the attic yet."

Ellie snorted. "It would serve you right if I had. How can you get anything done sleeping in this late?"

No use explaining how brutal her schedule had been. That she hadn't slept past sunup in three years. Reese squinted at the grandfather clock sitting in the foyer, but of course it wasn't working. Too bad. It was an exceptionally nice piece that she hadn't appreciated until now.

She used the elastic band she'd snapped around her wrist to pull her hair back. The chin-length bob barely made it into a ponytail. "How long have you been up?"

Ellie grinned, a broom in one hand, a blue chipped mug in the other. "Half an hour."

Reese grunted as she passed her sister and headed toward the smell of coffee. "Where are we starting?"

"I think the parlor. The kitchen is too daunting for this early." Ellie frowned. "Every cabinet is jam-packed."

"I kind of remember that. Lots of mismatched china, huh?"

"Yep. I hope I ordered enough boxes and packing material. Mr. Kent had the stuff stacked in the dining room."

Reese blinked at her sister, and told her, gratefully, "I'm glad you thought to do that."

"No problem. You've been busy." Ellie had already set out an extra mug. She filled it with black coffee, just the way Reese liked it, and got herself a refill.

Reese smiled fondly. Steady, dependable Ellie. Always there to pick up the slack. "I'll make it up to you. I promise."

"Knock it off, silly. Come on," Ellie said, and led the way.

The parlor drapes had once been an attractive emerald-green, they decided after a brief argument, but time and dust had turned the fabric the color of pea soup. God only knew what sort of critters lived within the sateen folds. Ellie used the broom to stir things up and warn any potential inhabitants to vacate. Nothing scurried across the dusty floor, so Reese braved her way to the gold cords, which fortunately still worked. A few tugs and sunlight flooded the room.

Luckily, the antique Chippendale furnishings hadn't suffered much abuse and would likely fetch a nice price at auction. None of the area rugs were salvageable, but that was of no consequence since they were of the cheap braided country-style variety.

Ellie leaned the broom against a powder-blue-painted wall and stared at one of the Old West prints that hung over an ornate mahogany table with curved cabriole legs. "I think this is a Currier and Ives original."

"It has to be a print." Reese went to join her and stared at the peaceful farm scene. "An original would be worth a lot of money."

"It looks really old."

Reese peered closer. "Hmm. It does. When did they start making prints?"

"You're asking me?"

"You're the photographer."

"Not this kind of stuff."

Reese shook her head. "I'm not sure we should be doing this."

"What?"

"Packing all this up and deciding what goes to charity and which pieces go to auction."

Ellie muttered in exasperation. "Come on, Reese, it has to be done."

"No, I'm not trying to get out of it. I simply don't think we're qualified to determine values."

Ellie nibbled her lower lip. "Damn. It never occurred to me that Grandma's things were worth anything."

"We were kids the last time we spent a summer here. Everything just seemed old and unattractive," Reese admitted.

"You'd think Mother or Dad would've warned us." Ellie laughed uneasily, and they exchanged knowing looks. Brad and Linea Winslow weren't horrible people, just lousy parents.

"Okay, so if we're agreed that we need more expert help…" Reese turned to her sister with a smile. "There's not much else to do today but—"

"The attic," Ellie finished, bubbling with giddy laughter, and ran for the stairs.

"Hey. No fair." Reese scrambled after her, three steps behind.

Ellie's much longer legs gave her the advantage, and no matter how hard Reese pushed herself, she made it to the third floor behind her sister. Both laughing and out of breath, they found the narrow stairs that would take them to the forbidden zone.

Only once had they been allowed to accompany their

grandmother into the cramped stuffy room when she'd gone in search of a photo album. The cobwebs and dust bunnies and creaking floor had been formidable, but the allure of an ornately carved chest and collections of vintage toys won their curiosity. They hadn't been able to explore as much as they'd have liked.

Something had spooked their grandmother and she'd quickly herded them out, warning them that the attic was forever off-limits. Nothing could have made breaching the boundary more appealing to curious eleven- and thirteen-year-olds. But that had been the last summer they'd spent in Deadwood. At the time they hadn't understood why, but in retrospect, they knew that Grandma Lily had begun her descent into dementia.

Ellie let Reese go first, a gesture she wasn't sure she appreciated. The dust and mustiness nearly overpowered her, throwing her into a coughing fit, but she found relief by shoving open the window facing west. It was small, the clouded glass scarcely providing enough light for Ellie to find the bare overhead bulb.

"Tell me again why we were so excited to come up here," Reese said between coughs.

Ellie sneezed three times. "If I end up on the floor at least I'll have a doctor to see to me. This is ridiculous."

"We don't have to do this." Reese pulled the neckline of her shirt up over her nose and mouth until the crisp outside breeze had a chance to circulate.

"It's getting better already." Ellie stationed herself near the open window and took several gulps of cool spring air. Then she turned toward Reese, but her fascinated gaze went past her. "Would you look at that."

Reese twisted around. In the corner, hanging on a seamstress's form, was a wedding gown. A very fancy one with lots of lace and pearls. Forgetting about the cloying air, Reese moved toward the dress. "It's beautiful."

"It couldn't have been Grandma Lily's," Ellie said, coming to stand beside her. "She was tall. That dress is tiny."

Enthralled, Reese ran the tip of her finger over the high, pearl-trimmed neckline. "It's in remarkably good shape, but it's really old. Maybe it belonged to her mother."

"Try it on."

"What?" Reese stared at her sister, strangely intrigued by the idea.

"I bet it's your size."

"Probably the closest I'll get to a wedding."

"Stop it."

Reese shrugged. It was the truth. They both knew it, but her lack of a love life wasn't a big deal. She'd made her choice. A career was important to her, besides the fact that she was picky about men. Overly so, she'd been told more than once. "Okay, I'll try it on if it's not too dusty."

Astonishingly, it wasn't too bad. Ellie readied the fragile dress, with only a couple of pearls coming loose by the time Reese wiggled out of her sweatpants and took off her top.

"This sucker is kind of heavy," Ellie said. "You should probably step into it."

Reese nodded and carefully did as suggested. Cringing under the weight, she sucked in her belly as Ellie struggled to button up the back. "I bet this is supposed to be worn with a corset."

With a grunt and a firm tug, Ellie secured the hook and eye at the top. "Let me see."

Reese gathered up the skirt, lifting the hem off the floor, and spun around. "What do you think?"

"You look awesome. Come see in the mirror."

A full-length mirror propped by a walnut easel stood in the corner by the window. Reese stared at her reflection in surprise. The dress was amazing. Charming and old-fashioned, with a high neck, long sleeves that came to a point just above her knuckles, and a cinched waist that left no room for a decent meal.

"I'm taking a picture," Ellie said. "Where's the camera?"

"Still in the car, I think." She couldn't take her eyes off the exquisite dress. The workmanship was stunning, from the intricate lace to the generous use of pearls.

"I'm going to go look for it and refill our mugs." Ellie stopped, her eyes narrowed. "Don't even look at that chest while I'm gone. I mean it."

"Not even a glance." She heard the stairs creak as Ellie went in search of coffee and camera. Spellbound by the reflection of the dress, Reese blinked. Why hadn't they seen this gown that time they'd come up here with Grandma Lily? She had so many questions about the dress that couldn't be answered now that Grandma was gone. It had to be really old. Was there a veil that went with it? Her gaze drifted to the trunk. But she'd promised Ellie.

She was about to turn back to the mirror when a bright white light flashed from the trunk and momentarily blinded her. She blinked a couple of times, until her vision cleared. Everything slowly came back into focus. The chest looked just as it had a few minutes ago.

Intrigued, Reese gathered the skirt in her hands and, making sure the hem cleared the scarred wooden floor, hurried to the trunk. The key was inserted in the lock and turned easily. Bracing herself, she leaned back and slowly lifted the lid.

A cloud of dust rose, spiraling up her nostrils, making her cough and sneeze. The haze dispersed and she wiped her watery eyes with the back of her hand, careful not to ruin the sleeve. She squinted until her vision cleared, to find a book lying on top of a pair of laced-up shoes and some trinkets. Ordinarily the latter would have been what captured her interest, but it was the book that drew her.

The once-blue jacket was old and faded to gray, she noted as she gingerly picked the volume up with both hands, worried about the condition of the narrow spine. Her attempted caution ended up making her clumsy, and she nearly dropped the book. Luckily, she recovered it before it hit the floor. A page came loose and she opened the book to inspect the binding. The 1910 copyright surprised her. She'd thought the publication was older.

With great care, she turned to the loosened page, her gaze riveted to the picture of an open wooden coffin. Propped up inside was a grainy photograph of a young dark-haired man, his eyes closed. The eerie image gave her a chill, and why she didn't immediately close the book she had no idea. She simply couldn't. Something about the handsome stranger pulled at her.

It was crazy; the man had been dead for over a hundred years. But a haunting familiarity gripped her, so soundly that goose bumps surfaced on her flesh. Her eyes went to the caption.

"Sam Keegan, 29, hung in the rear of the Deadwood jail, for stealing Mr. Hastings Barnett's horse on the 23rd of April last."

Below, an article explained the practice of photographing convicted criminals and displaying their pictures for the public as a means of deterring illegal activity. With a sudden sadness weighing down her shoulders, she looked again at the handsome face.

The dead man opened his eyes.

She gasped and blinked.

Sam Keegan stared back at her, the pleading in his eyes unmistakable.

"No." Reese stepped away and dropped the book. Again the white light flashed from inside the trunk, and she lost her footing. The gown tangled around her feet and she fell, clutching futilely at the air. Her head hit the floor with a thud, and then there was nothing.

## 2

THE STENCH WOKE HER. Stale tobacco and cheap booze and something else Reese didn't want to think about. Slowly she opened her eyes, to see that it was the cold, roughened hardwood floor that scraped against her right cheek. A cramp seized her twisted leg and she tried to stretch it out, but something restricted her movement.

She looked down in the dimness at the lacy white dress tangled around her ankles. The wedding gown. In Grandma Lily's attic. She took a deep, ragged breath and pushed herself up. But this wasn't the attic. How did she get down to the parlor? It looked different. The Chippendale sofa was the same, and the table with the claw-and-ball feet, but...

A cacophony of voices drifted in from a distant room. Raucous laughter. A man's booming demand for whiskey. The lively sound of a piano.

"Ellie?" She got up as far as her knees. Pain shot from the base of her skull and gripped her entire head. She sank back onto the floor and squeezed her eyes shut against the pounding, finding odd comfort in the scratchy wood pressed to her cheek.

"Well, well, look who finally woke up. It's the blushin' bride. Better get your ass up before Margaret takes a whip to you." Cackling accompanied the strange voice.

Reese lifted her head and peered out through slitted eyes. Two women stood over her, or maybe she was seeing double.

No, one was taller, thinner, her hair an unfortunate shade of red. "You being new and all, maybe Margaret won't have you beat for getting drunk without a customer."

Reese forced her eyes open. Both women were dressed in costumes, Old West designs. Not the chaste, old-fashioned kind, but something that a saloon girl might have worn. The shorter, curvier, blond woman's low-cut bodice barely contained her abundant breasts. She stuck the toe of her black, heeled boot out and nudged Reese's arm.

"You can't lie there all day," she said, her face creasing. "What's wrong with you, anyway? You sick? What happened to your hair?"

Was this a joke? Ellie wouldn't do this. Where was she? Reese opened her mouth, but nothing came out. She could barely breathe.

The redhead, who was dressed in what looked like a long nightshirt and thin beige stockings, crouched beside Reese. She had to be only in her early twenties, but time had been unkind to her. "You are sick, ain't you, honey?"

"I don't know," Reese whispered, noticing the burgundy velvet drapes that allowed in only a trickle of sunlight. A kerosene lamp kept the room from being too dark. "Where am I?"

The redhead stared for a moment and then frowned at the other woman. "Maybe we should fetch the doc."

She shook her head. "Margaret won't like that. This one ain't earned her nothin' yet. She won't wanna have to pay Doc, too."

The redhead still looked troubled, but she nodded. "Come on, honey," she said, grabbing ahold of Reese's arm and struggling to her feet. "You have to get up."

Reese didn't have much choice. The woman was stronger than she looked and all her tugging made Reese's head hurt worse. "I'm dreaming," she muttered as she was yanked to her feet, holding her breath against the sharp odor of the woman's unwashed body. "I'm going to wake up and everything will be all right."

The blonde and redhead exchanged wary glances.

"You ain't gonna get no more money out of them miners dressed in that gown," the redhead said. "Might be a good idea you go change."

"Flo and Mary, what the hell is keeping you gals? We got customers." The voice came from outside of the room. A woman's voice, hard and scratchy like a three-pack-a-day habit.

"Come on. Leave your dillydallying." The blonde grabbed Reese's other arm. "The old lady's in one of her moods today. You don't want to cross her."

Reese's head continued to pound as she let them guide her out of the room. She wasn't too keen on going with them, but she wouldn't find answers lying on the hard floor. The blonde, whose name was Flo, Reese learned, took the lead down a hall that was too narrow for the three of them. Mary held on tightly to Reese's arm, forcing her toward the voices, the sound of clinking glass and strange piano music.

The air was humid and stuffy, the musky smells horrendous, and just as Reese thought she might pass out again, they rounded the corner into a huge room. There were people. A dozen. Maybe two. Men. Women. Sitting on velvet sofas, or standing at a mahogany bar that stretched across the front of the room. One by one everyone stopped talking and turned to stare at Reese. Even the middle-aged, balding piano player abandoned his keyboard.

The only sound came from the ticking of a grandfather clock. Reese slowly turned her head. The clock looked a lot like Grandma Lily's.

A woman let out a loud bark of laughter and approached with an arrogant air that forewarned trouble. Dressed in crinkling red satin, her dark hair piled high, her pinched face framed with corkscrew curls, she drilled Reese with her small black, piercing eyes. "So you're the new girl?" Her gaze raked the wedding gown, and then she carelessly grabbed a fistful of the delicate lace. "What kind of foolishness is this?"

Reese jerked back, and the woman released the dress.

Mary gasped and quickly moved away, leaving Reese unsteady and teetering slightly.

The older woman's thin lips curved in a slow, evil smile. "A feisty one, eh? I'll fetch a good price for you. But make no mistake, you disobey me and I will have you whipped."

This had gone too far. Reese cleared her throat. Even if this was some crazy local reenactment, how had they produced those awful smells? "Who are you? What is this place?"

After a second of tense silence, a man yelled out, "You got a live one there, Margaret." Everyone laughed, and then some went back to their private conversations. The woman gestured with her hand and the man sitting at the piano resumed playing. Behind him, on the wall, was the same Currier and Ives print that hung on Grandma Lily's parlor wall.

Reese's stomach tightened into a knot. This was insane. Maybe she was the crazy one. She touched her forehead. No fever. She glanced around at the different women in various stages of undress, pandering to men wearing everything from starched-looking black suits to dusty Levi's and sweat-stained shirts. The place looked like a brothel straight out of a Western movie.

Her gaze went back to Margaret, who studied her with a combination of malice and curiosity. "They might be wearing their hair short like that back in the East, but that don't work here. You got to grow it out. Wear a bonnet till you do."

Reese took a deep breath. Until she could get a grasp of the situation, there was no use antagonizing the woman. She forced a smile. "I'd like to see that newspaper over there on the bar if I may."

"So you can read, huh?" Margaret frowned, apparently preoccupied with something near Reese's mouth. She pinched the tip of Reese's chin and lifted it. "You got good teeth."

Reese swatted her hand away. "Okay, that's enough. I need an explanation. Now."

Everyone within hearing distance lapsed into silence again. Margaret's eyes narrowed to dangerous slits. "I ain't got but one shred of patience left in me."

"That's more than I have." Reese sidestepped her and grabbed the newspaper off the bar. The date read 1876. She blinked. Her skin crawled. Impossible, of course. Someone had gone to an awful lot of trouble to pull off this joke. But she didn't know anyone like that. She spun around to scan the crowd for a familiar face. Even a stagehand, maybe, who'd worked on one of her parents' movies. Not that she knew many of the people in their circles, but what other explanation could there be?

A cowboy's sweaty, putrid odor reached her before he did. She slowly turned to face him. A bushy mustache obscured half his features. Although he wasn't much older than herself, his sun-ravaged, leathery skin had robbed him of youth. He got close, trapping her between himself and the bar.

"Kinda skinny, ain't she?" he said, while reaching into the waistband of his dusty Levi's.

She panicked, afraid he was going to pull down his pants and do God knows what to her. But he withdrew a small leather pouch and took out a gold coin.

"I reckon I'll have a go at her anyway," he said, passing Margaret the money and gripping Reese's arm.

Reese swore colorfully and twisted free. Margaret tried to block her path, but she was too quick. She gathered up the cumbersome skirt and ran out the double front doors into the blinding sunlight.

"DAMN YOU, SAM. You're really starting to piss me off. Where's my whiskey?"

"Now, Doc, I believe you've had enough." Sam hung up Doc's black coat on the hook behind the door of his small examining room. "The boys are down from the mines. You know it's gonna be rowdy in town tonight. How are you gonna patch anybody up if you're drunk?"

Doc sank into the wooden chair next to the cot used by his patients while he dug out bullets or applied mustard plasters, and laid his head back against the chipped wall.

"You ought to understand by now, Sam. I need a drink to calm my nerves. I can't work on anybody like this." Doc held out his shaky hand. He didn't have to fake it. His hands hadn't been steady since his wife had died of consumption two years ago.

But Sam knew that the man's demons went far beyond the helplessness he felt over the death of his missus. Him and Doc, they shared a long history. They shared the same nightmares. "Tell you what. I'll give you a drink, but I'm gonna hang on to the bottle."

Doc's dark brows drew together in a fierce frown. "I don't need a damn nursemaid. I need my whiskey."

Sam sighed. How many times had they had this conversation? At least once a week. You'd think a body would get tired and give in. Doc's, that is. Not Sam's. But this was his penance. "You stay here. I'll be right back."

Doc said nothing, just glared at Sam slipping out the door. He'd hid the bottle in a different place, because he had a suspicion Doc knew about the hole he'd dug under the front porch. Could be he was wrong, but he swore the last bottle of whiskey he'd hid had gone down an extra inch or two. Of course, Doc had been known to barter his services for a quart of applejack now and again, so he never stayed dry for long, no matter what Sam did.

Mostly Sam tried to keep his friend on the straight and narrow on busy nights when the boys tended to get riled up, and favored their guns over curses. That's when the blood spilled too freely, and if Doc saved one out of three he was doing good.

Sam trotted over to his livery across the street, curious at the commotion outside the Golden Slipper. Whatever had happened, the sheriff had been called, but since he was sweet on Miss Margaret it was hard to tell if he was hanging around outside because there was actual trouble. Sam hadn't heard any shots, so he wasn't going to worry about it. He briefly checked on the two newly boarded horses belonging to a couple of tinhorns staying at the hotel, and then grabbed the bottle of whiskey he'd tucked under his bed, behind his two extra shirts and a stack of books.

The stables weren't much when he'd bought the place. Still weren't. But he fixed them up as he could, mostly when he made some spare money helping Jacob, the town's blacksmith, who sometimes got more orders than he could handle. Lately, with more and more folks from the railroad showing up, Jacob sometimes worked sixteen-hour days. Sam himself didn't mind the extra work. He just didn't like so many people nosing around town.

For two years now he'd lived, worked, slept and ate here in the stables. Once in a while he'd take a drink at the Silver Nugget or eat a hot meal at the hotel. He'd stopped going to the Golden Slipper a year ago. The less he kept company with folks he didn't know, the better off he'd be. No, his life started and stopped between the stables and Doc's. Didn't matter if the situation he'd carved out here was to his liking. It was more than he deserved.

By the time he got back outside, the sheriff was gone. So was his worthless deputy. A few miners hung around the establishment, counting their coins or eyeballing their latest finds. Might be they were trying to figure out if they had enough for a bath, a meal and one of Margaret's girls. But other than that, everything looked peaceful.

Sam had reached the middle of the street when he saw Joe Weaver's boy kicking up dust, running hell-bent for Doc's office.

"I need Doc," the boy shouted as he got closer. "Where's Doc?"

"Calm down, son. What happened?"

The boy doubled over, trying to catch his breath. He planted his hands on the front of his thighs and looked up with a fire-red face. "It's Billy Ray," he panted. "He's behind the Golden Slipper and he ain't breathin'."

THEY'D STOPPED HUNTING for her. At least for now. Reese sat on the hard ground behind a wooden barrel, her knees drawn up close to her chest, the once beautiful white gown now caked with dirt and grimy from her sweaty palms. Her head had mercifully stopped pounding, but her pulse remained in overdrive and her body shook so hard her teeth rattled.

From her vantage point she could see the backs of two weathered wooden buildings, and farther toward the trees, a small boxy structure she imagined had once been an old outhouse. She desperately wanted to get a better glimpse of the incredible scene she'd glimpsed after escaping from Margaret. If she took another look she could prove to herself that there was no saloon called the Silver Nugget, no cowboys with guns slung low on their hips, no hitching posts, or horses with their heads lowered to troughs.

Everything had looked so real. Nothing made sense. It was almost as if she'd been swept into a time vortex and sent back over a hundred years. Of course, that was ridiculous. The possibility didn't exist. This was certainly an absurd but elaborate joke. There could be no other explanation. So why didn't she just stick her head out? Show herself and tell whoever was responsible that their fun was over?

She couldn't move. She wasn't certain she was even capable of standing. Hugging herself closer, she listened to the unfamiliar sounds and harried voices that loomed too close for her peace of mind. She was totally insane for buying into this charade. The sooner she put a stop to it the better, yet fear like she'd never known anchored her to the safety of the shadows.

Afraid to close her eyes, she rested her head back against the unfinished wood, stared at the clear blue sky and replayed the events of the afternoon. Grandma Lily's attic. The dress. The trunk. The photograph of the man—the horse thief. What was his name? Sam something. Oh, God. He'd opened his eyes. Or so she'd imagined. She'd fallen, and that's when everything had gone crazy. Ellie.

Where was her sister? She wouldn't have participated in this prank. She hated practical jokes.

Reese swallowed hard. For the first time she wasn't so sure this was a joke. Yet her scientific mind battled the fantastic idea that time could be manipulated. Whether by a freak twist of nature or technology…

A noise snapped her out of her preoccupation. It sounded like someone choking.

Without thinking, she leaned forward. She saw him standing in the alley through which she'd fled. A child, about twelve, bent at the waist. Alone. Gasping for air.

She hesitated, hoping someone would come along and help him. When he went down, she pushed herself to her feet, hearing the lace tear in her attempt to free her legs. She reached him in seconds, positioned herself behind him and slid her arms under his diaphragm. Two well-placed thrusts and a green marble flew out of the boy's mouth.

Sighing with relief, she released him. But he collapsed into a boneless heap in the dirt.

Reese crouched beside him and felt for a pulse, first at his neck and then inside his wrist. Life was there, but it was dangerously weak. She rearranged his head and shoulders, preparing him for CPR.

"What are you doing to that boy?" A stocky woman in a long dress and white bonnet barreled down the alley, shock and fear contorting her face. "Leave him alone."

"I'm trying to help him."

"You ain't helping him." The woman stood over them and peered down with horror in her eyes. "You're—you're a—God help us."

"Trust me. I'm a doctor."

The woman gasped in disbelief, then spun around and screamed for help.

Reese knew what would happen if she stayed, but she couldn't leave the child. Not when she could save him. But she had to act fast. He'd gone from red to pale to a pasty gray. Ignoring the hysterical woman, Reese placed one hand over the other, and with the heel of her right palm, started chest compressions, while silently counting.

Several more people rushed down the alley and gathered around her and the boy. They murmured and whispered, but no one tried to stop her. She mentally blocked them out and continued with her work, noticing that the child's color still wasn't good.

A man wearing a black coat and hat and carrying a leather satchel knelt beside her. His breath stank with the foul smell of cheap booze. "I'm the doctor," he said, eyeing her curiously before transferring his attention to the boy. "I'll take care of Billy Ray."

"Best you move aside, miss." A hand rested gently yet firmly on her shoulder.

She turned to the owner of the deep rumbling voice. Her own heart nearly stopped. It was the man in the photograph. It was Sam Keegan.

# 3

TOO STUNNED TO MOVE, Reese stared at the man. Tall, lean, dark hair, brown eyes. He looked like Sam Keegan, but he couldn't be….

"Ma'am, please." The doctor touched her arm.

She looked away from the mysterious man and shot a glance at the boy, who was deathly still, his gray pallor ominous.

"Sam," the doctor said quietly, and the dark-haired man took her by the shoulders.

She flinched under his touch, but was too shaky to rise to her feet, so she got on her knees and managed to move a foot away from the doctor and his patient. Somewhere in her foggy brain she knew this was the time to run, get away while the anxious crowd waited for the doctor to revive the boy.

But her attention went back to the doctor, who'd checked the child's pulse and sat back on his haunches with a resigned expression.

He sadly shook his head. "It's too late."

The crowd murmured.

"No." Reese roughly elbowed the man and, caught off guard, he fell backward. "No. It's only been a few minutes," she said, and resumed chest compressions.

Behind her a collective gasp rose from the crowd.

"What are you doing?" the doctor asked tersely.

"Says she's a doctor, too." It was the woman's shrill voice, and then a man muttered, "This ain't right. Somebody's gotta stop her."

"That so?" The doctor leaned close and spoke low enough for only her to hear. "You studied medicine?"

She ignored the boozy breath that fanned her cheek, and nodded curtly as she gave her all to administering the CPR. Hands gripped her shoulders hard, but she wouldn't stop.

"Let her be," the doctor said quietly.

She slid a look at him and met his puzzled blue eyes. His brows dipped in a frown, his wary gaze going back to the boy.

The child they called Billy Ray sputtered and coughed. His body jerked and he coughed again.

The crowd jumped back.

Reese sighed with relief, gave the boy a hand and pulled him to a sitting position.

The sudden deafening silence around her deflated the brief joy she'd felt. Her gaze went back to the man in the black coat, whose weary face expressed total disbelief.

"What did you do?" he asked unevenly.

"It's called CPR—cardio pulmonary resuscitation."

The boy pushed to his feet and dusted his hands together. "Why's everybody standing here?" he asked, looking around, his freckled nose scrunched up in confusion.

The doctor gave Billy Ray a cursory glance. "You're quite the lucky young man, son," he said, and then turned back to Reese, his bloodshot eyes serious and probing.

The woman with the white bonnet grabbed Billy Ray's bony arm and pulled him to her bosom. "She's one of those witches from back East I read about."

Another gasp came from the crowd.

"Hush, Mrs. Higgins." The doctor waved an impatient hand. "Explain this CPR."

Someone murmured something about getting the sheriff, and someone else agreed. Agitation spread like wildfire and had Reese struggling to get to her feet. She gathered the folds of the gown and lifted the hem, preparing for flight, and everyone's gaze went to her red-and-white designer running shoes.

Taking advantage of their apparent shock, she fled down the alley.

"Wait!" It was the doctor's voice. "Sam."

Just hearing his name, she stumbled and nearly fell, but then righted herself and ran around the corner. She didn't see the two steps leading up to the boardwalk. She hit the wood planks with a loud thud, causing pain to shoot through her right knee. Someone grabbed her arm. Without looking, she knew who it was.

Sam's hand tightened as he helped her up. "You hurt?"

She shook her head and then lowered her gaze to avoid the curious stares of two older women hurrying off the boardwalk and crossing the road. The truth was, she couldn't look at him, either. Not until she cleared the craziness in her brain.

"Where are you headed?" he asked, his hand still clamped around her upper arm.

"I, uh…" She tried to put weight on her injured knee and winced. "I'm not sure."

"You are hurt."

She could scarcely deny it, limping as she was. She chanced a look at him, met his whiskey-brown eyes, and her insides started to flutter.

"How about we head for Doc's office?" Sam paused and glanced over his shoulder. "You'll be safe there."

Reese swallowed and then nodded jerkily. How much choice did she have? She didn't want to end up back at

Margaret's. God, this was nuts. *If,* and that was a gigantic if, she had somehow traveled through time, how was she supposed to find her way back?

"Best you put this on," Sam said, and she turned to see him lifting a black coat draped over his arm. "This is Doc's." Sam's gaze briefly lowered to her breasts. "That marriage dress is a might conspicuous."

Reese slipped into the coat before testing her walking skills, because with her knee throbbing as it was, she feared she'd need all her attention to keep from falling on her face. Sam waited patiently, but his jaw was clenched tight and his gaze kept darting back toward the bordello. On Doc the coat came to mid-thigh, but on Reese's five-two frame the hem skimmed her calves.

Sam took her arm again, and she didn't protest. For all she knew he could be the enemy, but she was pretty sure Doc was curious enough about her CPR ability that he truly wanted an audience with her.

She and Sam walked to the end of the boardwalk, and if they received more stares she didn't know, because she kept her face forward and her back straight. Sam stayed quiet and that suited her just fine. She did wonder where the doctor was, though, and why he hadn't followed. Maybe she should be worried about that, but she was too drained.

Anyway, she'd sensed enough interest on the doctor's part that he'd make sure nothing happened to her, at least until she explained the principles of CPR. She needed somewhere safe to go where she'd have time to think. And if he was willing to hide her for an hour or so, she'd accept the offer.

"SIT RIGHT DOWN HERE." Doc offered her the only chair in the room and then dragged over a wooden crate that he kept his supply of bandages in.

She slowly sat down, her confused gaze shooting to the shelf of calomel, jalap, castor oil and plasters. When she spotted Doc's stethoscope and forceps, her eyes got bigger than a ten-dollar gold piece, as if she wasn't sure what she'd just witnessed. Funny thing, since she claimed to be a doctor.

"Sam, go get another crate for yourself," Doc suggested, while lowering his tall, thin body onto the wooden box, his attention on the woman.

Sam didn't want to sit. He leaned a shoulder against the wall, folded his arms across his chest and tried not to stare. Something about her bothered him. Even with the silly short blond hair she was a looker. Small, though, not much bigger than a child, but she wasn't that young. Closer to his own age, he reckoned, which meant she likely had a husband on her heels.

He studied the soiled marriage dress. Might be she'd run out on her wedding ceremony. That would be a fine thing to do to a man's pride. But whatever happened between her and her betrothed was none of his business. Sam sure didn't need trouble. Neither did Doc.

"What's your name?" Doc asked, the line between his brows deep with curiosity.

"Reese."

Doc smiled. "What's your first name?"

She couldn't seem to stop inspecting Doc's healing things, but then she met his eyes. "That is my first name. Reese. Reese Winslow."

Doc frowned, probably thinking the same thing as Sam. Strange name for a gal. She had to be from the East. "I'm Nathan Ballard. But everyone calls me Doc. That's Sam Keegan," he added, inclining his head in Sam's direction.

Sam nodded politely, but she barely looked at him. Seemed to want to look everywhere but. Fine by him.

"You say you're a doctor. I heard women were starting to take up the practice," Doc said thoughtfully. "Did you go to school?"

She blinked. "Of course." Her gaze went to Sam then, but only for a second before her eyes narrowed on Doc. "Didn't you?"

He noisily cleared his throat. "You must've gone to Women's Medical College of Pennsylvania."

Frowning, she slowly shook her head. "No, Harvard."

Doc laughed. "Harvard?"

"Yes, it's a fine school," she said defensively.

"Indeed it is." With his disappointment plain, Doc glanced at Sam, who knew nothing about schools, but could tell something about this Harvard had put Doc off his feed.

Or maybe he'd just figured out what Sam had already considered. That maybe this woman, pretty little thing that she was, wasn't right in the head.

She lifted her small, dainty chin. "My specialty is cardiology."

Doc smiled politely. "Are you hungry? Would you like something to eat?"

"Is this a joke? Please tell me this is a joke." She stood all of a sudden, went to the small window and pushed the faded curtain back to look outside. "Where's Ellie?"

Doc pinched the bridge of his nose, his hand starting to shake, and then peered at Sam. "Ellie? Sounds familiar. Is that Herman Miller's wife?"

Reese spun around. "She's no one's wife. She's my sister, and I demand to see her right—" Her voice broke off, her mouth still open as she stared at something on the floor near the head of the cot.

Sam cricked his neck to see. Five empty whiskey bottles sat neatly on the floor. A sixth one was half-full of amber liquid. He glared at Doc, who turned as red as a late summer tomato.

"I'm having me a drink and I don't wanna hear a word about it." Doc got to his feet and kicked the wood crate aside.

Sam pushed away from the wall. "Come on, Doc. Think that's wise? It's near sundown. You know what's gonna happen."

"What?" The woman wrapped her arms around herself, her eyes full of alarm. "What happens after sundown?"

Doc snorted. "They'll be coming down from the mines like mules in heat." He set out an unwashed glass and uncapped the whiskey bottle. "If they wanna spill each other's brains all over Main Street, not much I can do about it."

"Holy crap."

Sam and Doc both looked at the woman.

"This can't be real," she muttered to herself, plainly agitated. "It can't be."

She pushed a hand through her short hair, looked out the window again and then shook her head. "You don't seriously work on patients in this room." When neither man spoke, she added, "It's filthy, unsanitary, for God's sake."

"Look, ma'am." Doc poured a double shot of whiskey. "Can't say I wasn't impressed with what you did for the boy, but I don't take kindly to your high-handedness. I do my best here. This is Deadwood. Not New York City."

"I'm sorry." She didn't look it. "I shouldn't judge you." Her tongue darted out and swiped at her lower lip.

Sam's body reacted in a way that horrified him. Made his thoughts go where they shouldn't. Could be Mrs. Higgins was right about the woman being a witch. He crossed the room and snatched the whiskey bottle out of Doc's hand. "We had a deal."

"Sam," he said wearily. "Give me the bottle."

"Tonight. I can help." Reese ran her palms down the front of her lacy dress. "But I need a place to stay."

Doc snorted. "I've got just one cot and one room in the back. Sam, you can put her up in your livery."

Sam had to clear his throat before he choked. "I have but one cot myself."

"Plenty of hay." Doc smiled, and taking advantage of Sam's being dumbstruck, grabbed the whiskey. "Can't turn the lady out, Sam."

*Shit.*

The woman looked at him with those big, pleading green eyes the color of fine emeralds. There was fear there, no matter her bold words.

Before he could say anything, two loud shots came from the direction of the Silver Nugget.

He went to the window and saw that low-down Hank Lester and his two gunmen riding toward Doc's. "You claim you're a doctor. Looks like you'll get your chance to prove it."

THE DRESS WAS a hindrance, and Reese wished she had something else to wear. The long apron that Sam gave her helped keep the voluminous skirt from getting in the way too much, but the room was cramped and dirty. Reese hoped Doc was sober enough to handle whatever emergency came through the door. For a host of reasons, she doubted she would be of much assistance.

Her headache had returned and her racing thoughts weren't conducive to concentration. She mourned the comfort of believing that this was some kind of joke, even though the alternative was more than she could process. If she accepted the possibility that she'd actually traveled through time, then her objective was to discover how to get back. Her head pounded harder.

The commotion around her didn't help. Sam had kicked the wooden crate to the side, and while he picked up the chair she'd occupied, she peeked out the window. Two men had already dismounted and were helping a third man with a bloody shoulder and arm get down from his horse. They'd be in at any moment, and she was far from mentally or physically prepared.

"I think it's a shoulder wound," she said, spinning around to see Doc reaching for the whiskey bottle. *Great.* "We need water. Hot water," she amended, and when Sam frowned, she muttered, "I don't suppose you have a microwave."

Sam's frown deepened. "I'll get the water. But it'll take too long to heat."

"That better be for the patient," she said to Doc, wresting the bottle from him just as he was about to refill his glass.

His bloodshot eyes blazed. "Now, see here—"

"We'll need clean rags and bandages." She saw that Sam hadn't moved, but stood staring at her in bewilderment. "Water?" she repeated.

He grabbed a bowl and went through a narrow side door.

Doc's protest was cut short by the three men entering the office, one of them losing blood by the second.

The taller, steely-eyed cowboy, whose body odor had Reese reeling backward, pushed his way to the cot and roughly laid his friend down. The wounded man groaned in pain. Blood covered most of his shirt and seeped into his blue jeans.

"Slim took one in the shoulder, Doc." The tall man looked more disgusted than sympathetic. "Right next to the one you patched up last month. He ain't gonna be no use to me for a long while."

Doc just shook his head, eyeing the bottle Reese had placed safely behind her. "I'll see what I can do."

"Make it fast. Before the sheriff comes pokin' around." He frowned abruptly at Reese. "Who are you?"

"I'm a doctor, and you'll have to leave."

The man barked out a laugh.

"She's right, Hank." Doc rolled back his sleeves. "If you want us to work fast, best give us some room."

Hank glared at her, letting a short silence lapse. "Seth, wait outside."

Reese watched the other man open the front door in time for Sam to carry in the bowl of water. Hank stayed where he was.

"We're going to need more than this," she told Sam, and then glanced at Hank. "You, too. Out. Now."

Looking furious, his right fist clenching, the cowboy took a step toward her.

Sam blocked him. "Hank," he said quietly, but with a harsh expression that gave the other man pause.

Hank held his ground, staring into Sam's unwavering eyes, and then, with a foul oath, adjusted his Stetson and left the room, slamming the door behind him.

"Better watch your mouth," Sam said grimly. "We don't want trouble."

Reese doubted that was a problem for Sam. She stared at him, still digesting the subtle transformation from soft-spoken, polite cowboy to a man that she for one did not want to cross. Apparently, neither had Hank. She guessed he'd seen what she had, the lifeless, nothing-to-lose intensity in Sam's eyes that held more threat than a gun.

A groan from the injured man snapped her back to the

reality of the situation. She found a bar of what some might consider soap, and went to work scrubbing her hands, while uneasily watching Doc probe the patient's shoulder.

"Easy, son," Doc said when the man's upper body lurched from the cot, his anguished cry filling the room. "Easy now."

She looked at his pain-distorted face and realized he was young, probably still in his teens. Her gaze went to the large knife Doc had withdrawn from a leather sleeve, and she gasped. He couldn't possibly be thinking of using that.

"Sam, I need some help here," Doc said. He gestured with his head, and Sam positioned himself behind the young man and held him down.

"You," Doc said to Reese. "Hand me the whiskey." At her look of disapproval, he sighed. "It's for the patient."

Reese got the bottle and handed it to him. "You haven't looked at the wound yet."

"You just hold on, or you can wait outside, too." He glared, and then to her horror, tipped the bottle to his own lips.

Sam cursed softly.

"I can't operate with a shaky hand, can I?" Doc grumbled, and then held up the patient's head and forced some whiskey into his mouth.

Reese couldn't stand it another moment. She grabbed the cleanest rag she saw, and dipped it into the water. They had to clean the wound and get a better look at what they were dealing with. But no matter what they found, she knew that large knife wouldn't be appropriate.

Doc took another swig before relinquishing the bottle to Sam, and Reese gritted her teeth, knowing it was going to be up to her to get that bullet out. She cleaned the area the best she could and examined the wound.

"What other size knife do you have?" she asked Doc,

her attention remaining on the young man. "What method do you use for sterilization?"

After too long a silence, she looked up. Sweat had popped out on Doc's face. Bleary-eyed, he wobbled over to the shelf of remedies.

"Go sit down, Doc," Sam said. "The woman will take over."

Doc looked as if he didn't have much choice. He went to the corner and sagged against the wall.

Reese's gaze flew to the shelf, which seemed to be dominated by castor oil. Amazing that anyone survived. God, what a nightmare.

A loud bang sounded outside. Another shot. She met Sam's eyes.

"Best hurry," he said bleakly. "Reckon we might have a full house tonight."

# 4

WITH EACH PASSING HOUR, Sam's admiration for the woman climbed a notch. Tirelessly, and without a word of complaint, she treated patient after patient. Eight of them, by Sam's count. Even when the men eyed her with distrust and grumbled that they didn't want to be treated by no woman, she remained calm and determined. She hadn't lost a single man, either, which was more than could be said for Doc on any given Saturday night.

Sam glanced over at his old friend, who was passed out, broken from the nightmares and memories of that fateful day thirteen years ago. Doc did his best here in this hellhole, and if it weren't for him, Deadwood would have no doctor at all. That was saying something.

"Okay," she murmured, stepping back from the stranger she'd just sewn up. She used the back of her arm to wipe the sweat from her brow. "Try to stay off that leg. Keep the area clean and you should be fine."

The older man cringed as he slid off the cot and put weight on the leg that had been sliced by a knife, his dusty mining clothes sending up a cloud. Reese blinked, wrinkled her cute little nose and moved another step away. Sam handed the man his pants.

"Thank you, ma'am," the miner said, climbing slowly into his Levi's. "Thank you kindly. Best sewing up I ever got."

Sam waited until the man grabbed the doorknob, and then said, "Forgetting something, mister?"

The man frowned, and then sheepishly dug into his pocket and handed Reese a gold piece.

She accepted the payment and then tossed it on the shelf, just as she'd done with the rest of the coins and gold. She was a confounding woman, all right. Plainly not interested in money, unlike most of the gals Sam had met in his twenty-nine years. If he hadn't pointed out that Doc didn't get his castor oil and plasters for free, she would've let everyone walk out without paying so much as a dime. When Sam had asked her if she had any money of her own, she'd sobered up right quick.

For the first time all night, no one was waiting outside to get patched up. A true mercy, because she looked pale and tired. She hadn't eaten, and refused all but one small drink of water.

"I didn't think it was ever going to get quiet," she said, parting the curtains and peering out into the early morning darkness.

"Things settle down once the boys are too drunk to aim their guns."

She laughed, but her face was drained and she still had a small limp from her fall. If she fell asleep standing up, he wouldn't be surprised. "Some things never change."

In the corner, Doc stirred, muttering something Sam couldn't understand. Seven hours had passed since he'd had any whiskey. He had to be coming out of his drunken stupor.

Sam went over and shook his shoulder. "Doc."

He slowly opened his red eyes and squinted at them. "What time is it?"

"Past midnight. If anybody needs mending, you have to take over."

Doc blinked hazily at Reese, and then frowned at Sam. "Where you going?"

"To get the woman fed."

She let out a frustrated sigh. "My name is Reese."

Sam met her annoyed glare. "Yes, ma'am."

"And furthermore, I'm not hungry. Just tired." She pulled off the apron and pushed the hair away from her face, her whole body sagging as if the action took the stuffing out of her. "And don't call me ma'am," she insisted, her head lolling back before she slumped to the floor.

Sam reached her before she hit too hard. He picked her up in his arms and cradled her to his chest, taken by how fragile she was. The dress probably weighed more than she did.

"I should have a look at her." Doc struggled to his feet.

"She's just tired, is all. She's been working seven hours straight."

Doc's gaze went to the pile of bloody rags. "She worked on patients?"

"Yep. Did a fine job, too. Didn't lose a one."

Doc appeared unconvinced. "Anyone ask questions?"

"None of them seemed to be on speaking terms with the sheriff, if that's your meaning."

He nodded thoughtfully. "Where you taking her?"

"She can use my cot tonight."

"Maybe you'd better leave her here. Too many folks know about her now, and the sheriff not liking you and all. If she brings trouble, I can weather it better than you."

Sam shifted her slight weight, and then grabbed the extra lantern on the way to the door. "See you tomorrow, Doc."

Sam made sure no one was on Main Street before he crossed to the stables, even though they were situated at the far edge of town. Doc was right. Enough people knew about her, but he didn't need to announce her whereabouts.

If anyone asked, he'd tell them she'd disappeared in the middle of the night. But it wasn't as if she'd hurt Billy Ray. She'd saved the boy, so Sam couldn't see what business anyone would have with her.

*Reese.* Sure was a peculiar name for a woman.

He carried her past the horses to the small room that had been added on to the back of the stables where he slept and ate. The cot wasn't all that comfortable, but she was too whipped to notice. He wished that he'd picked up some, for the place was a mess. But there wasn't anything he could do about that right now.

After setting down the lantern, he kicked back the sheet with the toe of his boot and then gently laid her down, setting her head on the mound of straw he'd fashioned under an old sheet. She didn't budge and, worried, he pressed two fingers to the pulse at the side of her neck.

God Almighty, but she had soft skin. Smoother than fancy Chinese silk. Without thinking, he dragged his fingers down her neck to her collarbone. He'd never felt anything like it. A few of the ladies over at the Golden Slipper had skin that was soft and without a single callus, but nothing like this.

Realizing that he shouldn't be touching her, he jerked his hand back. Luckily, she didn't stir, her thick dark lashes resting against her porcelain cheek. He wanted to touch her again….

Abruptly Sam stood. He looked around for a clean sheet to throw over her. The last two nights he'd gone without a coverlet due to the recent warm spell, and truth be told, she was sleeping so soundly she wasn't likely to notice. Still, for his own peace of mind, he dug through his winter things and found a quilt Clara Bruin had made for him before she figured out he wasn't the marrying kind.

He laid the brown-and-beige patchwork over Reese, mostly so he would stop staring at the narrowness of her waist and the swell of her breasts. She was a fine looking woman, all right. Or maybe it had been too long since he'd visited the Golden Slipper.

No matter. He had no business eyeing her like a prized filly. He grabbed the lantern. He had to find himself a place to sleep. One stable was empty, though low on hay. But he was tired himself and the hard ground wouldn't keep him awake.

"Sam?"

He'd gotten as far as the door when he thought he heard her voice. Holding up the lantern, he peered at her dimly lit face. Her lids were heavy but her eyes were open.

"Where am I?" she asked softly.

"The livery."

"Is this your bed?"

He moved closer because he could barely hear her. "Yes, ma'am."

She smiled and then yawned. "Where will you sleep?"

"In one of the stables."

"On the ground?"

"There's lots of hay."

The corners of her mouth turned down. "You save me and I repay you by stealing your bed."

"You're the one who did the saving. I reckon Tom Bacon's gonna be building one less pine box tomorrow."

Worrying her lower lip with straight white teeth, she lifted her head. "Come closer."

He frowned, curious as to what she wanted, and moved nearer to the cot.

She reached out a hand, and he crouched down beside her, surprised when she touched his cheek. After trailing the tips of her fingers along his stubbly jaw, she traced the scar near his ear, the one he'd gotten from a broken bottle five years back.

"This isn't a dream, is it?" she whispered.

Sam gritted his teeth when she pressed her warm, soft palm to his cheek. She smelled better than a woman had a right to, and her feather-like touch lit a powerful fire in his belly that set his good sense smoldering.

"It's no dream," he muttered gruffly. "Best you get some sleep."

She quickly withdrew her hand. "Thank you, Sam. For everything."

He swung the lantern around as he got up so she couldn't see how the front of his britches had tightened.

OVER AN HOUR had passed since the sun came up, and Doc could see its brightness topping the distant trees. He left the window and poured himself a whiskey, the only sure cure he'd found for a hangover. After he'd downed two shots and his nerves began to steady, he started picking up the bloody rags and cleaning the ooze off the cot and floor. By all visible accounts there'd been a lot of gunplay last night. The senseless violence was hard to stomach, and he'd witnessed more than a soul should endure.

So had Sam. And his friend Jake. But neither of them had turned to spirits for comfort. Of course, they'd been little more than boys at the time of the massacre. They couldn't be held accountable, no matter what Sam thought. Doc had been full-grown. A man of nineteen. He'd known better, yet he'd blindly followed orders like a weak old woman.

He scooped up the damning evidence of his binging and dumped the empty bottles into a wooden crate. Next he gathered the instruments the woman had used last night, most of them not choices he himself would've made for gunshot wounds. Yet Sam had said the woman did good. If not for her efforts, men would've died last night. Like so many who had perished on his watch. Just like his sweet, angel-faced Martha.

God help him, he didn't want to think about his dead wife right now. Even after two years, guilt dug into him like the fangs of a rattler, spewing its venom and filling his body with unbearable pain.

In his haste to pour another drink he nearly knocked over his last whiskey bottle. He muttered a pithy four-letter word. That would be a fine thing. Losing his reserve, and having to beg Sam for each lousy sip. Doc slammed the bottle down on the counter, and that's when he saw the gold piece. Several more had been scattered behind a bottle of castor oil, as well as a few silver dollars. He picked up a double eagle and stared at it in disbelief.

Good God Almighty. Where had this bounty come from? Had the woman earned this last night? He never saw this much currency in a single day. Of course, not all his patients left his office on their own two feet. But why had she left it behind? Rightfully, it was hers to keep. Sam would likely collect the coins for her later.

His pulse quickening Doc swiftly pocketed a half eagle. That would keep him in whiskey for a while.

"Mornin,' Doc."

At the sound of Sam's voice behind him, guilt assaulted Doc. It wasn't his habit to take what didn't belong to him. But he had provided the instruments and bandages, he reasoned; that should earn him something.

"Mornin', Sam." Doc looked past him. "Where's the woman?"

"Best you call her Reese. She gets a might testy if you don't."

Doc noticed the slight upward curve at the corners of Sam's mouth, something a body didn't see much. "She still here?"

"Asleep, I suspect." He handed Doc a cup of steaming black coffee.

"She say anything about leaving?"

"Nope. She was dead-tired last night."

Doc sipped the strong brew even though he would have favored another shot of whiskey. "You say she did good last night."

"She surely knows something about healing." Sam went to the window and looked out toward his livery. "What do you make of her, Doc?"

"She's got spunk."

"Yep. Anybody ask about her?"

"If they had, don't you reckon I would've told you by now?" Doc snapped. Immediately regretting his sour tone, he put a hand to his throbbing forehead.

Sam slid him an irritated look. "I didn't force that whiskey down your throat last night."

"That I could never accuse you of, my friend."

Sam smiled, but just as quickly grew serious again. His chest heaved with the deep breath he took. "I've got a big favor to ask you, Doc."

"Go on."

Sam tilted his head to one side as if to relieve a kink, then shifted. Whatever he had to ask wasn't coming easy. "I suspect Reese has nothing to wear but that marriage dress. It's got some bloodstains on the sleeves. That's not so bad, but if a person is aiming to find her..." He shrugged.

When the full weight of what Sam was asking hit Doc,

he gripped the cot for support. Sweet Jesus in heaven. Martha's clothes. He had yet to touch a single thing that belonged to her. Her clothes and bonnets remained as they'd been the day she took her last breath. Her hairbrush and looking glass still sat on the small oak vanity he'd made for her the first year they were married.

"I know what I'm asking, Doc. It ain't easy for me. I expect it's hell for you."

Nathan swallowed around the lump that blocked his airway. "Makes sense," he said hoarsely, scarcely recognizing his own voice. "I've been meaning to clear out that room."

The sympathy in Sam's eyes was almost too much to witness. Doc turned away and drained his coffee, ignoring how the hot liquid blistered his lips.

"Need a hand?" Sam asked quietly.

"Get me a box." Doc headed for the back room. He'd pack up Martha's things, and then he was gonna go to the Silver Nugget and buy the biggest bottle of whiskey they had.

He'd hide the bottle good so Sam wouldn't find it. Try as he might, his friend couldn't erase the judgment in his eyes.

Him and Sam, they'd been to hell and back. They'd seen unspeakable things that burned a tragic image in a person's memory. And although his friend likely knew him better than anyone else, there was one thing Sam never could understand. Doc didn't drink when he wanted to drink anymore. He drank when the monster inside of him wanted to.

SUN STREAMED IN through the cracks and warmed Reese's face. She slowly opened her eyes. Her shoulder hurt, the pain burning a path all the way down her back along the right blade. She gingerly moved her arm and suddenly remembered last night. Remembered why she ached so much. Doc's small, antiquated office had received as many gunshot and knife wounds as an L.A. emergency room.

She sat up and immediately saw the bloodstains on the once beautiful lace. Her gaze went to the white antique bowl and a large-mouthed pitcher sitting on a small trunk. Except the bowl wasn't antique. Not yet. Yesterday hadn't been a dream. Oh, God. What the hell was she going to do?

She swung her feet to the bare floor, careful with the full, lacy skirt even though the dress was already ruined, and pushed herself off the narrow cot. Her mouth was incredibly dry, and she'd kill for a glass of water. Toothpaste would be equally nice, but she wasn't counting on it.

She got half her wish. On a three-legged wooden stool someone had left a smaller pitcher filled with water, and a tin cup. Presumably Sam, the tall, quiet cowboy who'd rescued her from the crowd and given her shelter.

The memory of him made her shiver. Not out of immediate fear, because he'd been kind and a total gentleman. And unlike most other men she'd come across here, Sam didn't carry a gun. But she remembered that look he'd exchanged with Hank last night, and she couldn't shake the feeling that this man could be dangerous. Especially to her. The photograph of him she'd found in Grandma Lily's attic seemed to have set all this insanity into motion. Had he somehow summoned her to cross time barriers to come to him?

Reese sighed. Obviously a night's sleep had done nothing to diminish her aberrant bout with whimsy. So much remained unexplained that yesterday's headache threatened to return. God, she could not think about this right now. First, she wanted to feel human again. Although under the circumstances that might be a stretch.

Finding that the large-mouthed pitcher had also been

filled, she pushed back her sleeves as far as they would go. Then she noticed a small container of white powder. She sniffed it and, realizing it was baking soda, giddily used it to clean her teeth. Soap and a towel had also been left, the latter a dingy white, but clean. The water and air were both cool but she didn't care. She washed up as best she could without taking off the dress.

Not only did she have nothing else to change into, but privacy was limited in the tiny room. Gaps between the boards allowed anyone passing by to peek inside, if so inclined. The only door was useless, the warped wooden panel so misshapen it didn't close correctly.

Yet this stark room was where Sam obviously lived. Besides the narrow cot and decrepit trunk, there were a couple of personal items, including a straight-edge razor and a comb. Yet no dresser or wardrobe for clothes, which made her curious. Tilting her head, she saw that he'd stashed some things under his cot. She crouched for a better view and was surprised to find two stacks of books.

She was about to reach for them when a noise came from beyond the door, and she turned her head, praying it was only Sam or Doc. After a moment's silence, she heard a horse whinny. *That's right,* she remembered, her pulse slowing. Sam owned the stables.

The light knock at the door recharged her heart, and she quickly stood.

Swallowing hard, she moved away from the cot, scanning the small room for a weapon. "Yes?"

"It's Sam."

Relief spilled through her. "Come in."

He pushed the door open with his boot. Today he wore a hat, which barely cleared the top of the door frame. He still hadn't shaved, and she kind of liked his rough-hewn look. His arms full, he silently walked past her and placed a box next to the cot.

"What's that?"

"Clothes." He stepped back and removed his hat, leaving an indention in his dark wavy hair. "Might be too big."

Reese picked up a blue skirt made of yards and yards of fabric. Her initial instinct was to balk, but she wanted out of the wedding gown so badly. Besides, she'd be less conspicuous dressed like the other women. "Where did you get these?"

He hesitated, and then said tightly, "Doc."

"Doc has a wife?"

Sam's mouth drew into a tight line. "She died."

"I'm sorry."

He nodded, already backing toward the door. "I got a needle and thread if you need them."

Sighing, Reese picked up a white shirt. Well, if she could stitch a patient, she supposed she could learn to mend a dress.

"I'll be out here. There's coffee on the stove." He turned for the door.

"Sam. Wait." When she had his attention, she showed him her back. "I need help with the buttons."

# 5

SAM STARED AT HER BACK, not sure what to do. He could tell she'd have trouble reaching the buttons, but it wouldn't be proper for him to see a respectable woman's corset or, heaven forbid, bare skin. But he sure wanted to. Was she as soft all over as her cheek and neck? Of course, asking for help with the buttons wasn't the same as inviting him to touch her.

"Sam?" She looked over her shoulder at him.

He cleared his throat, took a deep breath, set his hat back on his head to free up his hands, and walked toward her. She smiled and turned her head away. His gaze went to her waist, small and perfect, before her hips flared out. He knew she didn't wear a bustle and that pleased him. No sense in hiding the perfection she'd been given.

She lifted her hair off her neck. "Thank you for the clothes, by the way. That was very thoughtful."

He stared at the small patch of skin that had been hidden under her hair. Pale and without blemish. Soft looking. He wiped his clammy palms down the front of his Levi's. "Hold still now."

"They're only buttons. They won't bite."

Frowning, Sam found the first tiny pearl button, too small for his large, clumsy fingers. He fumbled with it before finally freeing it from the loop. There were a whole mess of the tiny pearls running all the way down to the curve of her bottom. He swallowed hard and forced his attention to the second one.

"Are you having trouble?" She looked over her shoulder again, and he met those pretty green eyes.

His fingers slipped. "I asked you to hold still," he grumbled.

"Sorry." She turned back around.

After some doing he unfastened five more buttons. He was getting a little better at the chore, especially with some of the looser pearls, but only when he kept his mind off what each freed button exposed. After two more, he saw the red silk. Was she wearing a corset, after all?

His gaze fixed on the skin above the silk. Golden, not pale like a woman's skin ought to be. He fumbled with the next button and again had to force himself to concentrate. About a minute later he'd released all the buttons down to her waist, where things got all fouled up again.

The dress parted, and he stared at the strip of red silk across her back. It wasn't a corset. Skin on the top, skin on the bottom… Like nothing he'd ever seen before.

His heart thundered, and no way on earth was he gonna get his fingers to work again. Sam lowered his arms, feeling as helpless as a newborn babe.

"What's wrong now?" She twisted once more to look at him, and the dress slid off her right shoulder, revealing a lacy red strap that went who knew where.

"Sam?"

He raised his eyes to hers. She frowned prettily, her eyes even greener than before. He shook his head. She talked funny, dressed peculiar and wore her hair too short. She had to be from back East. Those gals who came from New York and Boston were a puzzle. "I think

I've done all I can do," he said, his voice scratchier than a new bar of soap.

"What do you mean? Are the buttons stuck? I won't be able to get this dress off." She tugged at the right sleeve and then turned all the way around, and his heart damn near stopped altogether.

The red strap ended at the top of her bosom. Some scarlet binding covered her breasts, but not by much. He suspected he should be looking elsewhere, but he couldn't seem to make himself.

Reese laughed. "Haven't you ever seen a bra before? Oh, well, maybe you haven't." She reached behind herself to the buttons, her breasts thrusting at him.

He should leave, but he couldn't move his feet. Just stood there like a halfwit, his brain powerless to form a single thought.

"There." She sighed, bringing a hand around to hold up the front of her dress, the fitted waist going slack. "I have another favor to ask."

He took off his hat and held it in front of his fly. "Ma'am."

She shook her head in disgust, but he suspected that was only because he'd called her ma'am. "The boards aren't flush and I'm afraid someone might see inside."

His gaze went in the direction of her free hand, to the gaps between the planks. "We're at the end of the line here. No one comes this far unless they want to board their horse, and then they come to the front."

She wrinkled that pretty little nose of hers. "I'm not exactly popular around here. If someone gets curious…"

He caught her meaning. "I'll put up a board or two."

"Thank you."

He paused for a moment, wondering if he should ask about her plans for leaving. Then stiffened in shock, when that thought weakened his knees. Before he could think again, he heard the sound of hoofbeats, which slowed as they approached.

"Someone's here," he said. "Best you keep quiet."

The solemn way she nodded made him nervous. They needed to talk. If she was running from a husband or anyone else, he should know. Sam made sure the warped door closed as well as it could, and then set his hat back on his head as he strode out to the front.

The sheriff was riding toward him, his beady eyes keen with curiosity as he scanned the stables and haystacks. Sam didn't much care for the man. He was more crook than lawman, but he kept some order and mostly stayed away from the livery. Sam wondered what brought Sheriff Ames this way. He hoped it wasn't Reese.

"Mornin', Sheriff. What can I do for you?" The words weren't all out of his mouth when from the corner of his eye he saw the bedroll he'd left in the empty stall. He moved quickly, hoping to cut the sheriff off before he saw it and started wondering.

"Nearly full up, ain't you?"

"Yep. Got room for only one more."

The sheriff craned his neck, trying to look past the large wood stove Sam used for heat and cooking. "Is that coffee I smell brewing?"

"Sorry, Sheriff, it's just about gone," he lied, wishing the man would speak plain and move on. He wasn't one for paying social calls. At least not to Sam.

Ames reined in a foot in front of Sam. "I'm looking for a woman. A stranger. Traveling alone, I reckon."

The hair on the back of Sam's neck stood up. He searched his mind for the right reply and carefully met the man's shrewd eyes. Did he know about Reese's doctoring work last night? Most of the men she'd patched up had been miners or ranch hands. None of them had anything to do with the sheriff.

Sam shrugged. "I haven't seen anyone suspicious. But no one comes back here except to board their horse."

The sheriff's cold gaze stayed on his face, making him sweat. What in the hell kind of trouble had Reese brought on him and Doc? Shit, too many people had seen them with her.

"Doc had a friend visiting yesterday," Sam volunteered. "Another healer." He forced a laugh. "I never met a woman doctor before."

The sheriff narrowed his eyes and sat up straighter in his saddle. "So you did see the stranger?"

"Well, she's no stranger to Doc. So I didn't reckon that's who you were looking for."

Sheriff Ames's lips thinned. "I don't need you to do my thinkin' for me, Keegan."

"No, Sheriff, I wouldn't do that," he said evenly, tensing when the man pulled up on his rein, about to turn his horse around. "She was a looker. Blonde, green eyes. Too bad Doc got so stinkin' drunk that he run her off."

The sheriff stopped in his tracks. "She's gone?"

"Yep. Before sunup."

Frowning, he picked his Stetson up and pushed a hand through his thinning hair, then reset the hat on his head. "She keep a horse here?"

"Nope."

"How did she leave?"

Sam shrugged. "I'm headed to Doc's now," he said, real calm like. He and Doc had to get their stories straight fast. "Maybe he knows."

Sheriff Ames snorted. "Old Doc's over at the Silver Nugget. He won't be making much sense for a spell."

Relief mixed with disappointment. The miners were still in town and as soon as they woke up, there was bound to be more violence. But he should've known Doc would be looking for comfort. Going through Martha's things had to weigh heavy. Sam hoped Reese was worth that.

"The woman you're looking for...who is she?"

"A runaway whore."

Sam's belly clenched. "Wish I could help you, Sheriff."

With a knowing smile, Sheriff Ames drew his horse in a wide circle and looked down the alley on the side of the livery before cantering back toward town.

Sam stayed rooted to the spot. Reese was a whore. The strange fancy underthings made sense now. So did her lack of modesty. She hadn't given a second thought about asking him to help her undress.

A whore.

Nothing wrong with a woman trying to keep a roof over her head, he told himself. Not a damn thing. He cursed under his breath, and went to join Doc at the Silver Nugget.

THE SKIRTS AND DRESSES were all too long by a good three inches, as were the sleeves, but the bodices and waists fit pretty well. Since Reese finally figured out there would be no handiwork with a needle and thread in her near future, she chose a dark blue skirt that she rolled up at the waist until the hem cleared the floor, but still obscured her running shoes. She had to forgo the complementary white blouse for a drab brown one, fearing her red bra would show through. The more she blended in the better.

After folding the remaining clothes and finding a place for them near the cot, she examined the ruined wedding gown, checking each loosened pearl, the different lace patterns. As sad as it was that the beautiful gown and exquisite workmanship had been damaged, that wasn't her chief concern. The dress was her only link to Grandma Lily's attic. More importantly, to the twenty-first century. The key to returning home had to be here, in the dress somewhere. She just couldn't see it.

She checked her watch, abruptly realizing she'd have to tuck the gold Rolex away, and wondered what was keeping Sam. She'd vaguely heard him talking to someone earlier, but that had been over an hour ago. She didn't dare step outside. Not by herself. As much as she wanted a cup of coffee, she stayed perched at the edge of the cot, her gaze glued to the warped door.

Just as she thought about snooping through the books she'd seen stacked under his cot, she heard the horses neighing. Which either meant Sam was back or she was about to find herself in deep trouble. Or maybe it simply meant the horses were restless. Nevertheless, she put her hand on the straight-edge razor she'd found earlier and now kept in the folds of her skirt.

A brief knock sounded, and then the door opened.

She sighed with relief when she saw Sam. Tucking the razor into her skirt pocket, she got off the cot. "I was starting to worry."

He closed the door behind him, then gravely looked her up and down. "The sheriff was here."

She pressed a hand to her stomach. "Hunting for me?"

"Should he be?"

"You heard that woman yesterday. She thought I was a witch."

Sam studied Reese carefully, disappointment in his brown eyes. "How did you learn doctoring?"

"In school."

His dark brows rose. He didn't seem to believe her. "Back East?"

She hesitated. She knew what he meant. Regardless, Harvard was located on the East Coast. "Yes."

"Why did you come here?"

She moistened her lips. "That's a difficult question to answer."

One side of his mouth went up in a mocking slant. "How did you get here?"

Crossing her arms over her chest, she hugged herself, as it suddenly chilled. "I could use some of that coffee you offered earlier."

He looked as if he was going to ignore her request, and then grimly turned and left, leaving the door ajar. She moved so that she could see where he was going. Perhaps straight to the sheriff. The strange way he was acting concerned her. Something had obviously happened in the past hour to make him suspicious of her, but how could she possibly explain the events of the last twenty-four hours? He wouldn't believe her. She didn't believe it herself.

Just as troubling, she had no idea what to do next. If the dress was the key to normalcy, it wasn't opening any doors. For all she knew, returning to the bordello would be instrumental in her getting home. In the meantime, she had no money, and no way of moving around town undetected. One thing for sure, no matter what, she'd need Sam's help.

Between the back room and stables was a big potbellied stove where Sam stopped and crouched with his back to her. When he finally stood, he had a cup in his hand. After ducking out of sight for a moment, he headed toward her once more.

Reese quickly moved back to where he'd left her,

dismayed at the weakness in her knees. Perhaps he was about to kick her out on her rear…. She breathed deeply, trying to maintain her composure.

He entered the room and glanced over his shoulder before closing the door, and then thrust the cup at her as though he thought she was contagious. Her fingers accidentally brushed his hand, and he hastily withdrew, as if she'd infected him.

"Thank you." She wrapped her cold hands around the warm cup and took her first sip. Thick and strong, the coffee coated her mouth like motor oil, and she choked back a shriek of disgust.

She didn't want to appear ungrateful, or hurt his feelings, so under his watchful eye, she pretended to take a second sip.

Suddenly, he closed the distance between them, and she flinched, anticipating an assault. But he walked past her to Doc's wife's clothes, stacked neatly in the box beside the cot. He snatched a white bonnet and brought it to her. "You should wear this."

He was close enough that she got a whiff of whiskey on his breath. That shocked her. It was still early in the day, and she knew how he felt about Doc's drinking. She set the cup on the three-legged stool beside the pitcher, and accepted the bonnet with a shaky hand. He seemed to notice and looked away.

"Thank you." She'd really thought he was going to strike her, and considering that he'd been drinking, and what she knew about him being a horse thief, she was probably lucky he hadn't. "I guess women cover their heads most of the time."

He gave her an odd look. "Your hair is too short. You'll get noticed."

Her hand automatically went to the hair brushing the side of her jaw. It was no longer damp, and without the artistry of a flatiron, thick dreadful waves were putting too much spring in it. "I guess I should pull it back."

Except she didn't have any pins or an elastic band. She could use one of her shoelaces, but that could present another problem. She spied the wedding gown at the foot of the cot. Parts of the hem had come loose, and she could tear off a small strip of lace. She set down the bonnet while she found a piece that would do the least damage with its removal.

After she tied her hair back and placed the bonnet on her head, she turned for his appraisal. "Better?"

He frowned, staring toward her chin. "That's not right."

She touched her throat and peered down. "What?" After a stretch of silence she glanced up at him.

He visibly swallowed, and with his gaze fixed somewhere between her breasts and chin, he gestured with his head. "You've got skin showing."

"Oh, right." She'd left the top three buttons undone, but quickly fastened each one now, until the high, scratchy neckline irritated her skin and felt as if it would choke her. "How do I look?"

He said nothing, but his disapproving gaze went to her arms.

She groaned, then pushed down the overly long sleeves she'd rolled up, finally cuffing them at her wrists. The upside was that she could wear her watch again. She'd been worried about keeping it in the skirt's roomy pocket and losing it. For now, though, she left the gold-and-diamond watch right where it was, because she didn't think Sam was quite ready for one of the decadent marvels of the future.

After a quick visual examination, she tugged up her

skirt again and slowly spun around for his inspection. "How do I look now?"

Sam took a long time to check her out, his eyes darkening a couple of shades. "You'll pass."

She grinned. "For what? A woman?"

He didn't smile back. "A respectable one."

Reese's temper sparked, but she tried to tamp it down. Getting angry would get her nowhere. This was a different time, different morals. No matter how ridiculous or old-fashioned they seemed to her.

"Here."

She stared at his outstretched hand, fisted so that she couldn't see what he was holding. She opened hers, and he dropped some coins and two gold pieces into her palm.

"These are yours. From last night." He moved closer to the door. "A stage will come through around three."

With dread, she said, "You mean a stagecoach."

He nodded.

"You're kicking me out." Panicked, she followed, clutching his arm. "Why?"

He tensed, but didn't push her away. "There's plenty for passage, a hotel and a hot meal or two once you get where you're going."

"What did I do?"

"Nothing. You did good." He tentatively cupped his hand over hers, his callused palm scraping her skin. "You did what Doc couldn't. We're both grateful."

She blinked rapidly, hoping to keep any stray tears at bay, terribly afraid she'd embarrass herself, because she never cried. Tears didn't help. They only made a person look weak. "I don't understand."

He awkwardly patted her shoulder. "Nothing wrong with whoring. A woman's gotta make a living, but if I—"

She reared back, jerking away from his hand. "Whoring? What are you talking about?"

"I don't blame you for running. Margaret's a hard woman, but she and the sheriff—well, I can't hide you anymore. Doc and I don't need any problems."

"Sam, I'm not a whore. I never saw Margaret before yesterday. I'd never even heard of her."

His brows dipped in suspicion. "Yeah, well, I heard that two of Margaret's new whores arrived on the stage yesterday. Now one's missing."

"I'm not a whore," she repeated. "I'm a doctor. You know that, Sam. You saw me work on those men last night."

"That's a fact," he said, obviously confused. His gaze ran down the front of her blouse. "You wear whore clothes under there, and you don't mind a man helping with your buttons."

Reese sighed. She was not ready for this. After what she was about to tell him, she was more likely to end up in a nuthouse instead of the local bordello. "Sam, I think you'd better sit down."

# 6

SAM DIDN'T DRINK WHISKEY much, and he wished he hadn't downed two shots with Doc. This woman was confusing enough without spirits muddling his brain. She wanted to talk, and he wanted her gone.

Truth be told, he didn't want her gone all that much. She looked real pretty with her face scrubbed clean, and he kind of favored her hair wild and free. And if he lived to be a hundred, that image of her in the red lace binding would never leave his mind.

"I have horses that need watering," he said gruffly. "Best you speak your piece and then get ready for the stage. I'm sure Doc won't mind you taking some of Martha's things."

She moved toward him, and it took all his gumption not to turn tail and run. Especially when she touched his arm with a trembling hand, her eyes dark with fear.

"Sam, I swear to you that I'm not a whore. I really am a doctor. And I'm not crazy. At least I don't think I am. Even though I'm about to tell you something that is so fantastic you won't believe me."

He frowned, curious as all get-out, and hoping this wasn't some kind of trick. The way her lower lip quivered and her slender fingers curled around his arm made it hard for a man to think straight. "I'm listening."

Slowly, she lowered her hand, clasped it with her other one, lacing her fingers together. "I'm not from here."

Sam stared, not sure if he should be mad at her foolery or pity her.

"That's obvious, I know. What I meant is that I'm not from this—" The breath left her in a whoosh. "Oh, I—" She briefly squeezed her eyes shut. "I'm going to ask you one more time and then I swear I'll never bring it up again. Is this a joke? Is someone playing a prank on me?"

"You'll miss the stage," Sam said, and turned to leave.

"Wait." She grabbed his arm, and he stopped but wouldn't look at her.

She swept around to face him, the pleading in her green eyes enough to make a man do things more foolish than listening. "Have you ever heard of someone traveling through time? Jumping from one century or even decade to the next?"

"In books?"

"In real life."

Sam sighed. "Maybe I should get Doc."

"He'll never believe me, either," she groaned. "I can't believe it myself."

"Yesterday. You fell—"

"I know. I thought of that, but I only hit my knee. Anyway…" She gestured with her hand toward the stool and cot. "I couldn't possibly imagine all this. I was a miserable history student. I don't even like Western movies." Her eyes widened slightly. "No offense."

Sam didn't know what the hell to think. By now Doc likely wouldn't be much use. Maybe after he slept off the whiskey. "You haven't eaten. I've got some biscuits—"

"Look at these." Reese pulled up the hem of her skirt so that the funny looking red-and-white shoes showed. "Have you ever seen anything like these?"

Except his interest didn't rest on the strange shoes. She'd yanked the front of the skirt all the way up to her knees. She wore no stockings. His heart slammed in his chest. Slender yet curvy, her bare calves were silky smooth and hairless. He'd seen a woman's legs before, but only those belonging to whores. In the Golden Slipper they walked around in underwear a lot, to tempt and save time. But Reese was different. He'd started to think she was a lady. He could barely swallow.

"Look." She balanced on one foot, lifted the other and showed him the patterned sole of the shoe. "Have you ever seen anything like that before? Look at the detail," she said, pointing to the fancy, even stitching.

He squinted for a better look. Damn if the red-and-white material didn't look like leather. "Sometimes it takes awhile for the new styles to get here from back East."

She let out a strangled laugh and set her foot back on the floor. She stumbled, and he caught her arm. Her bones were tiny and fragile, and as much as he found that he liked touching her, he loosened his grip.

"All right," she said excitedly, and reached into her pocket. "What about this?"

He stared in astonishment at what was in her outstretched palm. Gold gleamed and sparkled. Not like the rough, sharp pieces of gold the miners brought into town. This was all polished, nice and pretty.

She turned it over and he blinked. It looked like some kind of timepiece. Much smaller than a pocket watch. The tiny clock was attached to a band. In a circle around the clock gemstones sparkled like stars in a midnight sky.

"Diamonds?" he murmured to himself. Maybe. He'd seen one only once, years ago.

"Here. Take it. Look closer." Reese shoved the timepiece at him. "It's called a wristwatch. They're made in Switzerland by a company called Rolex."

"Switzerland? In Europe?" The workmanship was so fine he was afraid to touch it.

"Yes, but they make watches everywhere now. Even in China."

He lifted his surprised gaze to her. "Chinamen make these?"

She smiled. "Not exactly like this, but yes, they make watches that go around your wrist. Clocks, too."

Sam frowned at the perfectly carved ridges all the way around the band. Too small to fit a full-grown person's wrist, even hers. That's how he knew she was lying. But the finish…how could anyone make gold this smooth and even? He was tempted to pick it up. Measure its weight. Maybe it wasn't real gold.

She pinched at something and the band parted. "See? This is how it works."

He looked closer and saw that it had stretched so she could slide it over her hand. Once it was in place on her wrist, she snapped something that tightened the band. She straightened her arm for him to see. A shaft of sunlight creeping through one of the cracks in the wall set the gem-stones to sparkling.

"Have you ever seen anything like this?" she asked.

He shook his head. "But I've never been to Switzerland."

Reese sighed. With two fingers, she pressed the side of her temple, briefly closing her eyes. When she opened them, she stared at him with curiosity. "How do you know about Switzerland? Did you study about Europe in school?"

"I've never been to school."

Her eyebrows went up. "Not at all?"

"Nope."

"You have books…." She gestured toward the cot, which riled him some. The books weren't in plain sight.

"I can read."

"Did your mother teach you?"

Sam took off his hat and hit it against his thigh, making her jump. The woman didn't know when to keep her mouth shut. What was wrong with her that she'd ask a stranger so many personal questions? Even if he ever had a mother or father, what made her expect he'd want to talk about them? "That timepiece work?"

"Yes."

"The stage leaves at three," he said, and left the room before she started shooting off her mouth again.

REESE CAREFULLY HID the wedding dress under the cot behind Sam's clothes and books, adjusted her skirt to make sure the running shoes were concealed, and then rearranged the white bonnet to hide her hair, and fortunately, half her face. The stables were quiet, save for the occasional neighing of a horse. She listened a minute longer before yanking open the misshapen door.

No sign of Sam. Or anyone else, thank goodness. A restless horse whinnied in the nearby stables, startling her, but she took a deep breath and ventured over the threshold toward the smell of burning wood and strong coffee.

Besides the back room, which she realized was nothing more than a poorly constructed add-on to the livery, there was a cavernous space with a dirt floor and high dilapidated roof that had to leak buckets when it rained. But the area did its job separating the living quarters from the stalls, and housing a huge pot-bellied stiove where Sam kept a kettle of coffee heated. Next to it was a pile of logs, a rickety-looking chair and a stump that probably served as a bench. Against the wall was a sideboard on which sat an iron skillet, a big black pot and two tin cups. Sam's version of a living room and kitchen combo, she thought wryly.

After that, the livery started in earnest. Basic tack hung on the wall to the left behind a small buggy with a missing wheel. Several feet away a pitchfork leaned against a narrow set of steps that led to a half-story loft, jutting out over the rows of stables that lined both sides of the shoebox-shaped building. Despite the dirt floor and the hay strewn about, Sam kept the place surprisingly clean and smelling no worse than the stables she's frequented as a young girl.

Satisfied that it was safe to do so, she moved closer to the heat, rubbing her palms together, trying to get them warm. The air wasn't nearly as chilly as when she'd woken this morning, but nervousness always made her hands and feet cold.

She smiled, thinking about how Ellie used to tease her when they were kids. Science or math exams had always been a breeze for Reese, but when it was time to cram for history or English, she had worked herself into a bundle of nerves, certain her ineptitude in those areas would prevent her from being accepted to medical school.

Ellie never doubted Reese's success for a moment. They'd often stayed up until midnight, Ellie rubbing Reese's cold hands, making her hot chocolate and quizzing her until neither of them could stay awake another second. A girl couldn't have a better sister than Ellie.

Reese sniffed. Would she ever see her sister again? She moved closer to the fire until her skin smarted from the heat. Feeling sorry for herself would get her nowhere. She had to stay focused.

Except she had no idea what to do next. She wouldn't be getting on that stage, that was for sure. Her stomach rumbled, although she wasn't really hungry. That was another sign of nerves: her appetite always disappeared. But she hadn't eaten in well over twenty-four hours and she knew better than to let herself get run-down.

A white napkin had been spread over a tin pan and she lifted the corner of the cloth and peeked underneath. There were two golden-brown biscuits about the size of her fist. Sam had offered them to her earlier, so she didn't feel bad about snitching one now.

She bit into the hard dry roll, fearing for her teeth. If Sam cooked his own food it was a miracle he wasn't ema-ciated. Definitely not the case. She'd felt his arms, and he was in fine shape. Muscular without being obnoxiously so, and had she seen him at an L.A. restaurant, his shoulders were broad enough to earn a second look.

Reese thought back to the many movie sets she'd visited over the years, and she had to admit there was no better actor to play the lead in a Western. Sam was exactly what everyone expected a cowboy hero to look like. Tall, a few inches over six feet, lean, rugged without being scruffy. He had dark, wavy hair and intense brown eyes. And if there was such a thing as a perfect butt, the man had it.

Despite the fact that she had enough of her own problems, his close relationship with Doc really had her curious. He practically babysat the man. Lucky for the town. She cringed at the thought of Doc's craving for booze and the detriment it was to his practice. But whether Sam's sympathy was for his friend, or for his unsuspecting patients, Reese was counting on Sam's compassion to help her find her way home. He knew the town, he could move about freely, while she couldn't.

At least for now.

The picture of him in the coffin popped into her mind and made her shudder. Sam, a horse thief? It didn't make sense. Was that why she was here? To prove that he hadn't done what he'd been accused of doing? But that didn't make sense, either. He was one man. How many innocents had been wrongly hanged through the centuries?

The sound of a horse trotting sent her scurrying toward the bales of hay stacked in the corner. She ducked behind them and clenched the rock-hard biscuit she still had in her hand. Sarcastically, she figured she could use it as a weapon if need be. Keeping perfectly still, she listened as the horse and rider stopped at the entrance to the livery.

"Hello? Anyone here?" It was a man's voice. He hadn't called Sam by name so she hoped he was merely a customer. "Hello?"

After a tense silence, she heard footfalls and then Sam's deep rumbling voice. "Afternoon, mister. What can I do for you?"

"I need my horse boarded."

"Got one stall left."

"Good. Good." He'd apparently dismounted, judging by the annoying screech of leather rubbing on leather. His voice differed from the ones she'd heard since yesterday. More crisp, perhaps citified. "I'll be staying at the hotel. Three days, maybe four."

"He's a fine animal," Sam said quietly.

Imagining his long lean fingers stroking the side of the horse brought a flush to her skin, a sudden yearning that made her breasts tingle. Her inappropriate reaction startled her. Yeah, Sam was hot, but she was in too much trouble to be distracted that way.

"Yes, he is. You take good care of Goliath and there'll be an extra dollar in it for you."

"I take good care of all the horses, mister," Sam said with a faint trace of resentment in his tone.

"Yes, I heard. Good man. I'll be at the hotel." Reese heard a clink of coins, and then the man added, "The name's Barnett, by the way, Hastings Barnett."

She knew that name. She'd read it in the caption. Hastings Barnett was going to accuse Sam of stealing his horse. For that, Sam would hang.

Reese's knees gave out, and she sank to the dirt floor.

HAVING HEARD THE NOISE coming from behind the hay, Sam hurriedly walked the man toward Main Street. Barnett plainly wasn't from around these parts, most likely from somewhere back East. But Sam figured if that was Reese making the racket, better no one saw her, not even a stranger.

There'd been enough talk of the runaway whore over at the Silver Nugget this morning. Some claimed she was a witch, others reckoned she was a spy for Stanley Hopkins, who was opening a new brothel at the other end of town. Margaret was certain that she was her mail-order whore from back East, who'd accepted stage fare to come West and now would rather find a husband than work.

Wrong or right, Margaret's belief was enough to get the sheriff involved, or else she'd make him start paying to go upstairs, like every other man who found pleasure at the Golden Slipper.

Sam took Goliath to his stall and then went to check behind the bales of hay. Reese sat huddled there on the ground, staring up at him, her small heart-shaped face whiter than newly fallen snow.

The relief that seeped through him because she hadn't left, even though he'd told her to, gave him a shock. She meant trouble. Plain and simple. He needed her on that stage and not hiding in his livery next time the sheriff came poking around. "You're gonna miss the three o'clock."

"That man who was just here…how long did he say he was staying?"

Sam frowned at the peculiar question. "Three or four days."

"Oh, no." She made no move to get up.

"Why?"

She opened her mouth, but nothing came out. He saw the biscuit sitting on the straw beside her. She hadn't eaten much of it, only a bite. After her hard work last night, she had to be weak. Maybe that had caused her crazy talk.

"Here." He took her hand to help her up. Her palm was smooth and soft, without a single callus. She hadn't done much outside in her life.

She struggled to her feet, and to his amusement, kicked at the folds of the skirt in a most unladylike fashion. When she finally steadied herself, she blinked at him, disbelief on her face. "You just smiled."

Sobering, he released her hand. "You can still make it if you hurry. The stage is at the hotel."

She sighed. "I'm not leaving, Sam. I know you don't believe what I told you, but it's the truth. That means I can't leave Deadwood until I find out how to get back to my time." She drew her lower lip into her mouth and then added, "I've been thinking about it and the key might be tied to my grandmother's house. The place is over a hundred thirty years old, which means it exists now and should be somewhere near town."

Sam stared at her, not knowing what to say. He wished Doc would get here. Unless he was too drunk by now, but Sam calculated he'd caught him in time. Doc had certainly been fascinated by Reese's far-fetched time-traveling story. He was about the only living soul Sam had the gumption to pass on the tale to. Mostly because he hoped Doc could help her.

"What are you thinking, Sam? That I'm crazy? I don't blame you."

He felt the heat climb up his neck, and turned away from her. "Doc's going to want to talk to you. Best you go back to the room so no one sees you."

"Thank you."

"Don't thank me," he grumbled. "I still mean to get you on that stage tomorrow."

She laughed softly and touched his arm. He didn't want to look at her, but it was as if he couldn't control his body, and he turned toward her. She rose up on tiptoes, tugged at his arm until he got her meaning and lowered his head slightly. She stretched up higher and kissed him warmly on the cheek.

His insides quaked. Like the time he'd gotten too close to one of the mines on exploding day. His hand went to the spot she'd kissed. He hadn't shaved in days. No telling how bad his scratchy whiskers felt under her full, soft lips.

Could be it was his imagination, but she looked a might out of sorts herself. Color stained her cheeks, and the tip of her tongue swept her lower lip. Her hand tightened on his arm and when she tilted her head back to look at him, the bonnet slipped, uncovering her shiny blond hair. He desperately wanted to feel its silky smoothness between his fingers, and forced himself to step away before he made a damn fool out of himself.

"You ought not to kiss a strange man like that," he said in a hoarse voice.

She gave him a smile that could melt stone. "You're not a stranger, Sam. You're my hero."

He stiffened. The woman didn't know what she was talking about. What would she say if she knew the truth about him? That he was a killer. A cold-blooded son of a bitch who had snuffed the life out of husbands and fathers and brothers. He'd left countless orphans across three states to fend for themselves. God only knew what had become of them. Maybe they'd all ended up like him. Heartless. Miserable. Wondering why he bothered to take his next breath.

Damn her for reminding him what a bastard he was.

"Sam?" Her face full of worry, she touched his arm again.

He stared at her small, fragile hand, knowing he could crush it with one squeeze. He'd never hurt a woman before. And he sure didn't want to start now, so before he picked her up and threw her onto the stage, he brushed by her and headed toward Main Street.

He wasn't sure what the hell to do about this woman. One thing he did know. He was no fucking hero.

# 7

SHE COULDN'T JUST sit there and hope Sam returned soon. In fact, he'd looked so angry Reese wasn't sure he would come back. At least not without the sheriff. She had no idea what she'd said to set him off, but he'd changed into a different man right before her eyes. His face had darkened, his fists had seemed to involuntarily clench, and his murderous glare left its mark in her queasy stomach. She replayed their last conversation twice, but still didn't get it. If anything, she'd complimented him. He looked as if she'd slapped him across the face.

The bigger problem was now he wasn't about to help her. She set the bonnet back in place, making sure her hair was completely tucked beneath the crisp white cotton. The blouse's voluminous sleeves covered the gold watch, and the long skirt brushed the ground and hid her running shoes. Now if she could only remember not to lift the hem, and still stay on her feet.

Two of the horses neighed as she passed the stalls. Goliath was one of them. She knew because his stall had been empty before Hastings Barnett showed up. Reese also knew horses, and the animal was truly magnificent. She'd been given riding lessons and a sweet-natured roan for her thirteenth birthday. She'd found that she loved riding and even won several competitions.

The rigors of college and then medical school had precluded extracurricular activities, so she hadn't ridden in years, but she still recognized an exceptional horse. She stopped to stroke the side of the bay gelding's velvety face. He snorted and nuzzled her hand.

"I'm sorry. I wish I had an apple for you," she said, and it took only seconds for him to lose interest. She smiled sadly. "You are beautiful. Is that what's going to tempt Sam?"

She moved away, shaking her head. Why would Sam steal this horse? Or any horse. He seemed to have a good business here, and then there was Doc. Sam obviously cared about the man too much to up and leave him. But what did she really know about Sam? His abrupt change in attitude and manners were proof enough that she knew little of him.

At the entrance of the livery she stopped to make sure no one saw her walk out. She inched around the door frame, angling her head first, surprised to see how far they were from the actual town. Her second surprise was the large crowd on Main Street. There had to be a hundred people out there. Both men and women swarmed the boardwalks on either side of the street, some walking purposefully, others leisurely visiting or gazing into shop windows. Several little boys played tag on the street, kicking up an appalling amount of dust.

Reese studied the scene with initial dismay, but then quickly realized that a crowd could help her blend in. Yes, there were more people who might be curious about her, but if she kept her face averted and stayed close to the storefronts, maybe she could make it to the other end of town, or Grandma Lily's house, whichever came first.

Of course, it made more sense that it wouldn't be in town, that it sat on the outskirts just as it did in her own time, but she had to try. She took a step into the sunlight, just as a sudden thought struck with such force she nearly ran back into the livery for cover.

The bordello. Some of the furnishings. The Currier and Ives print. There had been an undeniable familiarity. Why hadn't the idea occurred to her before now?

Because it was silly. She shook her head, checked her bonnet and hurried toward the boardwalk a block away. The Golden Slipper was definitely located in town, while Grandma Lily's house was situated over a mile away from the tourist trappings. The geography and street plan of Deadwood couldn't have changed that much.

She approached a young couple carrying groceries, and quickly averted her gaze, focusing on the window of the local newspaper office. They might have a list of residents. She couldn't go in and ask, but maybe Doc would be sober enough later to help out. Maybe even Sam would have cooled off. That last incident still puzzled her, but she couldn't dwell on Sam. One tiny mistake and she could end up in the sheriff's office.

After passing the barbershop, the telegraph office and a shop advertising laundry service, she recognized the alley where she'd hidden yesterday. Across the street were the hotel, saloon and general store. She felt her pulse race, knowing she was nearing the Golden Slipper and that horrible Margaret. Reese stopped to gather her wits, pretending interest in a yellow ruffled dress displayed in the window of a seamstress shop.

She inhaled deeply and then forced her feet to move in the direction of the bordello. Unless she crossed the street, she had to pass the place in order to see what was on the other side of town. Since leaving the boardwalk would only call attention to herself, she stayed on course and prayed no one from the Golden Slipper would recognize her.

Bawdy laughter and the cloying odor of stale tobacco and cheap booze drifted out the door. Luckily, heavy velvet drapes shuttered the windows, blocking the view of both the customers and people on the street. That was the only reason she felt safe stopping to stare at the building.

Air seemed to whoosh out of her lungs. The Golden Slipper and Grandma Lily's house looked remarkably alike. There were obvious differences, such as the lack of a porch, but the basic architecture was the same. The off-center door, the large, triple windows, even the bay window on the left, jutting from the eat-in kitchen. She would have to step out into the middle of the street to see if the small second-story balcony existed, as well as the Victorian-style turret that was part of the attic, but she wasn't willing to expose herself like that.

She glanced across the street and saw that people were beginning to stare curiously at her. A seemingly respectable woman standing idly outside of a bordello would naturally attract attention. She gathered her skirt, remembered the sneakers and promptly released the fabric. Before she could take a step, someone put a hand on her shoulder.

She jerked away, the reflex having more to do with the man's foul odor than the actual touch. Spinning around, she faced him, and glared in warning. His long stringy hair hadn't been washed in weeks, and his wild reddish beard looked as if it hid an army of roaches. The two missing front teeth made for a charming grin.

Wicked amusement glinted in his watery blue eyes. "Look here, honey. My gold is as good as the next man's."

"Your what—? No." She stepped back. "No. I don't work here."

"I like my women spirited." Grinning, he reached out a bony hand and, through the cotton, pinched her right nipple.

She gasped and stumbled backward. "You stupid son of a bitch. Touch me again and I'll break your damn hand."

The older man chuckled and took a silver dollar out of his pocket. "Yep, you'll do just fine."

He made another move for her, and loath as she was to touch him, she grabbed his wrist and twisted it behind his back until he yelped. She'd taken several self-defense classes and had done some kickboxing as an undergrad, but she backed off, not wanting to draw any more attention.

"Why, you little bitch." The man turned toward her with a meanness that alarmed her, and she drew back her arm, ready to lay him out.

Someone stopped her with a hand on her forearm and another at her waist. She twisted around, to be drawn against Sam's broad chest. His grip on her arm tightened in silent reproach before his gaze went to her assailant.

"Old man, you best not be bothering my wife," he said in a quiet but stern voice.

"Your wife?" The man narrowed his gaze at Reese. "She ought not be idling alone in front of Margaret's place like a common—"

"Mister," Sam interrupted, in that low warning voice that brooked no argument.

Reese opened her mouth to have her say, but Sam glared down at her. "Honey, shut up," he said, and pressed his warm, firm lips to hers.

She whimpered deep in the back of her throat, but he got his way. She couldn't have said anything if she wanted to.

Abruptly, he released her. The bearded man had already disappeared. Sam pulled his hat lower over his eyes, and with one arm around her waist, steered her back in the direction of the livery.

Remarkably, there didn't seem to be many people on this side of the boardwalk. They tended to gather closer to the general store and the saloon. She didn't kid herself, though. Several people had seen the commotion, but Sam had been careful to keep his voice low so that no one but the old miner could've heard his claim.

Still, being seen with her was enough to get him in trouble, probably the reason he promptly released her. She didn't argue with his forcefulness, just stayed by his side and kept walking. As much as she hated guns, she hated more that the other man had one and Sam didn't. If anything had happened to him because of her…

She shivered at the thought and wrapped her arms around herself. But it wasn't cold, far from it. The morning chill had given way to a sticky heat. That was partly due to the massive amount of clothes a woman was expected to wear, with barely any skin showing. It made her wonder how many people had died of heatstroke back in early times.

Then again, maybe the heat flash had more to do with the kiss. Ridiculous, because as far as kisses went the encounter had been brief and quite chaste. Mentally reliving the feel of Sam's lips against hers would last far longer. Reese swallowed. One lousy kiss meant only to shut her up. She had no business reacting, or giving it another second's thought. Especially not with the danger she was in.

As soon as they stepped inside the livery, she stopped and turned to him. "I have to go back there," she said, raising a restraining hand at his look of angry disbelief. "Not right now—I understand the mess I may have caused. But it's my grandmother's house—the Golden Slipper. I'm almost certain."

Sam frowned. "I've been here over two years now. That place was built last year."

"No, later it gets sold, I'm guessing, and somehow my family buys it or—" Frustrated, excited, she pushed the stifling bonnet off her head and fluffed out her hair. "I don't know what's going to happen, but I'm pretty sure my grandmother ends up with the house. I was standing in the attic right before I passed out and—" The sudden look of pity in his eyes stopped her cold. "Forget it. I don't expect you to believe me."

She fidgeted with the bonnet and unfastened the restrictive top button of the high-necked blouse, which pressed against her throat.

He glanced over his shoulder, then gestured for her to keep walking. "Go to the back before someone comes poking around."

"If it's too difficult to hide me…if that scene I caused brings the sheriff around…" She took an anxious breath. "I don't blame you if you give me up."

"Sunday afternoon. He's visiting Margaret. He won't want to be disturbed."

"Oh, good." Reese sighed with relief.

As they walked side by side toward the back room, her shoulder brushed Sam's arm. She'd accidentally touched him before, although this time it was different. Another flash of heat made her skin tingle. She gave him a sidelong glance but saw no reaction. This was so crazy. She was tired, that's all.

They got to the room and he pushed open the ineffective door. The sun seeped in through one of the gaps in the wall, throwing a shaft of sunlight across the cot.

Sam frowned. "I'll go put up that board now."

She crossed the threshold and then spun around to look at him. "If the sheriff did find me, what would he do with me?"

Amusement flickered in Sam's brown eyes. "Throw you in jail."

She folded her arms across her chest. "You think that's funny?"

The corners of his mouth twitched. "I reckon Sheriff Ames might find you're too much trouble to keep in his jail."

"Really?" She liked men with a sense of humor, but not when the threat of her being locked up seemed too real. A thought flashed through her mind. "Wouldn't he give me to Margaret?"

The humor left Sam's face. "Yes."

She paced the small room, trying to think. "That would get me into the house," she murmured to herself.

He grabbed her arm and forced her to face him. His harsh, forbidding expression made her flinch. "You want to be a whore?"

"No, of course not." She moved her arm, finding his grip painful, and he abruptly released her. "I wouldn't do that. I would—" She cleared her suddenly parched throat.

"What would you do, Reese?" he asked quietly.

He'd never used her name before, or if he had, not like this, his tone a caress that slid over her skin and warmed her insides.

She met his intense gaze. "Why did you kiss me?"

He looked nearly as horrified as she felt for impulsively uttering the words, and then his expression went blank. He rubbed the back of his neck and looked pointedly at the gap in the wall. "I'll fix the crack and then make supper."

Like him, she was more than willing to ignore the foolish question. "Sam, I know I've already asked for so much, but what I really would like is a bath." She glanced around the room, already knowing there was nothing to accommodate her. But there had to be a way. Maybe he had a tub behind the hay. She didn't care where it was. She was hot and sticky, and it had been too long since yesterday's shower. "Is that possible?"

He nodded once, his gaze briefly touching her breasts. His nostrils flared slightly. "I'll heat some water."

"Thank you." She felt frustratingly helpless as she watched him leave the room. Offering to make their meal was out because she didn't think she could handle the wood stove, or making anything from scratch, for that matter. She was more a microwave and frozen dinner kind of gal.

Today was Sunday, he'd said. Yesterday at Grandma Lily's house it had been Saturday. They were on the same calendar, at least. But did that mean anything? Other than the fact that she had an appointment tomorrow to meet with a hospital administrator to discuss her new job.

Groaning, she sank onto the edge of the cot. What would happen when it seemed that she'd fallen off the face of the earth? She couldn't imagine how her sister had reacted to finding her missing. Poor Ellie. Tears welled and Reese ruthlessly blinked them away. She needed to keep her wits about her. If she stayed calm and focused, she was certain she'd find the answer that would get her home.

A pounding behind her made her jump. She twisted around to see that the gap in the wall had been repaired. There were several other small openings, but nothing she couldn't live with. Someone would have to work hard at being able to see inside, and with no window, she welcomed the small amount of light the shoddy workmanship allowed.

At least now she could get out of the suffocating clothes. She imagined it would take Sam a while to heat the water, although she hoped he didn't get it too hot. What she really needed was a dip in her pool. She sighed from the pleasure of simply thinking about such a luxury, and unbuttoned her blouse, which she then quickly stripped off. Next she unlaced her shoes and toed them off. The skirt was easy to unhook, and she slid the yards of blue cotton down her thighs.

She bent over to pick up the skirt, and heard the brief knock. Before she could take cover, the door creaked open.

SAM FROZE IN HIS TRACKS. At the sight of her near nakedness, his heart thundered. Not just her back, but her legs were that light golden color. But that wasn't what kept him powerless to move. The same red silk that bound her breasts stretched across her hips in a narrow strip, but left most of her buttocks showing. He'd never have imagined it. The skin was golden there, too.

She slowly turned toward him, and his gaze went straight to the red silky triangle that covered her woman's place. She swooped the skirt up and held it against her body.

Her tongue darted out to wet her lips, and she held the skirt closer to herself. "I'm sorry. I thought you'd be a while."

He swallowed, willing his hardening cock to go down, anxious to put the wood tub between them. But the old trough was heavy and he had to drag it through the door, not sure it would make it past the narrow frame. He always took his baths near the stove so he didn't have far to carry the water.

The trough wouldn't move easily but he favored fighting with it over having to look Reese in the eye. He should be the one apologizing for surprising her. Or might be it was best to ignore the whole situation. He didn't have much experience being around women. Not one who was a lady. Whores were bred different.

He finally pulled the trough into the room close to the

cot. Reese backed away. He was kind of hoping for another look at her fine fleshy buttocks, but he forced his mind to veer from that line of thinking. Bad enough he'd been ungentlemanly, and he still couldn't get his cock to ease up.

With his eyes cast downward, he said, "The water should be ready soon."

"I can help bring—"

"No." He made the grave error of looking at her. She still had the skirt drawn to her body, but the top part of her bosom was in plain view. He inhaled deeply, trying not to stare at the plump mounds of golden flesh.

Without another word, he headed for the door, and when he got on the other side, closed it as tight as he could behind him. If he had his druthers, he wouldn't lay eyes on her again till mornin'. The woman was gonna make him as loco as old man Wilson, who'd taken to howling at the moon every time it came up full.

Hoping to dull the ache in his loins, Sam checked on the water he was heating, and then tended the horses. He still had to muck out the stables, look in on Doc and fix their supper. The day was near gone. In three hours the sun would set and the boys would be at it again. Wouldn't take them long to get liquored up, get separated from their gold by fast dealt cards, and then try to settle their differences with a gun. He hoped Doc would be up to the task of sewing the stupid bastards up.

Reese would do the mending, Sam knew, and she'd do a better job than Doc, but that upped the risk of her getting caught. He thought back to what she'd said about the sheriff handing her over to Margaret, and his blood boiled. Didn't she understand what Margaret would make her do for her keep? No one was gonna listen to her crazy story about being from another time. Talk like that might even

ruin her chances at earning whore money. Margaret would
have her whipped.

He tested the water, his temper growing just thinking
about the way that old miner had put his filthy hands on
her. It was plain she hadn't put on any of the petticoats Doc
had given her. Damn it. A man could get the wrong idea
about a woman not wearing a petticoat. Didn't Reese
understand that?

Not that he liked the notion, but tomorrow he'd help her,
even if that meant going to the Golden Slipper and poking
around. He didn't expect he'd find anything, but if he could
ease her mind that there was nothing here for her, might
be she'd move on.

Damn it. For two years he'd lived here in peace and
quiet. Not a soul but Doc knew who he was, or about the
evil he'd done. No one nosed around. Even the sheriff had
let him be. Until Reese came.

Sam hauled up one of the buckets of heated water, and
just knowing he was about to see her, felt his groin start to
ache again. She sure had soft lips. But right as rain, the
woman was gonna get him hanged.

# 8

REESE DIDN'T CARE about the rough, scratchy inside of the tub, or that the soap had an odd odor and a grainy consistency. Well, that wasn't true, she did care a little bit, but she was just so glad to be sitting in an actual bath. She hadn't realized how much her muscles ached from the fall

Reese laid her head back on the strips of toweling Sam had thoughtfully provided, closed her eyes and thought about her parents. Their devoted attention was one thing that had eluded her. They loved her, of course, she knew that, but they loved the spotlight more. They loved the publicity and the money and the way studios bowed to their demands.

How much of her success was attributable to them? The television gig, possibly, but the rest? How much had come her way simply because she was Brad and Linea Winslow's daughter? Oddly, she'd never considered that possibility before, and she didn't like it. No, not so odd, really. When had she ever had this much idle time to think? Her life was a total whirlwind, sweeping her from one engagement to the next. She worked hard, too hard to be denied her own yesterday—two fans, in fact, the first in Grandma Lily's attic. She appreciated the warm water that eased some of the ache, aware that it wasn't easy to come by.

Sam had made several trips, carrying two heavy buckets, to fill the tub. She'd offered to help twice, but his only reply had been a dark scowl and an averted gaze. She hated that he was so angry with her. He'd been nothing but kind, despite the fact that he probably wanted to kick her out on her ass, and she didn't know how to repay him. Although she had an idea that disappearing out of his life would be all the thanks he wanted.

She wanted that, too. More than anything. She simply didn't know how to achieve that end. Never in her life could she recall feeling so utterly helpless. What she'd wanted, she always got. Schools, dates, grades, the right clothes, an enviable sports car, a house on the beach, the perfect career. Everything had come easily. Not to say she hadn't worked hard, but still, she'd been lucky, she knew. Incredibly lucky.

Sadly, even to her parents. Would they miss her? When they found out she'd vanished, would they fly back from Spain or Monaco or wherever they happened to be? She rather doubted they would. Maybe after she'd been gone a month.

Ellie, on the other hand, would be frantic. She'd probably hired a private detective by now.

When the loud knock came, Reese knew that, like the last two times when he'd come to fill the tub, Sam wouldn't open the door until she gave permission. However, unlike before, she was already in the water, with no means to cover herself. There were no suds to block his view. The best she could do was take the coarse strips of towel from behind her head and float them over her body.

"Come in," she called, her heart picking up speed. Not from fear. It was that damn kiss that still had her worked up.

He opened the door, his gaze carefully averted from her nude body beneath the water as he carried in two more buckets. She didn't understand. He'd already filled the tub to the brim.

At her questioning look, he lifted one of the buckets, which she now saw was empty. "The water's gotten cool. I mean to take some out." He jerked his head toward the other bucket. "Put in more heated water."

Her lips parted, but she couldn't speak. She'd given him nothing other than grief, yet... Now she knew for sure that she was overly tired. She swallowed around the lump in her throat. Afraid the tears would come, she quickly sub-merged her head, then surged back up out of the water and wiped her face with her palms.

"Thank you," she said, her voice shaky. "Here. I'll scoop it up."

He handed her the empty bucket, his expression a wary mixture of frustration and confusion. Then he turned his back while she filled the container. She got on her knees, then tried to stand, hoping to be able to set the bucket outside the tub. She was in pretty good shape because she always made time for cardio exercise and weight training, but once it was full, she could barely lift it out of the water.

She noisily cleared her throat and slid back down to her knees. Even though she floated the towel strategically, he would inevitably see more than he should. That didn't bother her, but it might him. "Um, Sam?"

"Yep." He kept his back to her.

"You'll have to turn around so you can help me lift this bucket out of the tub."

Slowly, he swiveled around. His body jerked slightly when he saw that she was kneeling with her shoulders out of the water, the bucket the only thing blocking his view of her naked breasts.

His strong, tanned throat worked with his swallow.

"I know this is awkward," she said. "But I'm sure you've seen a woman's breasts before."

His mouth tightened; other than that his expression gave nothing away as he reached for the bucket handle. She'd planned on crossing her arms over herself as soon as he grasped the pail and pulled it out of the tub. But his taciturn mask annoyed her and ignited a perverse streak of stubbornness that had gotten her into a jam on a couple of occasions.

She'd seen the hunger in his eyes earlier when he'd walked in on her. She'd also seen the bulge at his fly. His stupid, silent indifference didn't fool her. So what. These were different times. He'd started it. She hadn't asked him to kiss her and send her mind in foolish directions.

Reese stayed right where she was, her arms at her sides, her breasts visible and bobbing slightly in the water. His biceps bunching beneath the tan shirt, he lifted the heavy bucket, and his gaze went straight to her breasts. He seemed transfixed, frozen, even as he muttered something under his breath.

"I think you'll have to dump the warm water in, too," she said, reminding him to move. "I won't be able to do it myself."

"What?" His heated eyes slowly met hers, and a dull flush crawled up his throat to his face.

He quickly looked away and set down the filled bucket, and then picked up the other one. Stopping, he slid his long, lean fingers into his breast pocket, his gaze staying on his boots. "I got this from Doc. Belonged to his wife," he said, thrusting a small square packet at her.

Their fingers brushed and he yanked his hand back so fast water sloshed out of the bucket onto the floor.

She hid a smile. "What is it?" As soon as she asked the question, the pleasing scent of lavender drifted up to her nose.

"Sweet salts," he said, his eyes still averted. "You put it in the water."

"Thank you, Sam." She was so touched by his unrelenting kindness, her voice broke.

His gaze shot to her then, regret darkening his eyes before he looked away again. "I won't be bringing in any more water," he said gruffly, and dumped what he had into the tub.

Delicious warmth spread around her. "Do you want to take a bath?" she asked impulsively.

He frowned, his dark brows dipping in bewilderment as he reluctantly cast another look her way. "Ma'am?"

She bit off a nervous laugh. She wasn't sure what she meant, either. If he wanted to join her, it would be a horribly tight fit, but she wouldn't refuse. The mere thought of his naked body rubbing against hers made her skin tingle and her nipples ache.

"It's a shame to waste all this water." She tried not to look, but she couldn't help it. The front of his Levi's stuck so far out it was impossible not to stare.

"Supper will be ready in half an hour," he murmured, and sped through the door so quickly he forgot the other bucket.

HE'D BURNED THE BACON. And the biscuits. Sam crouched by the stove and pulled the iron skillet away from the fire with disgust. She was a confounding woman. He didn't understand her one bit. She liked trying his sorely strained patience, that was a given.

Damn her. He rubbed his fly but found no relief. Looked like he was gonna have to go to the Golden Slipper and spend some of that money he had socked away. The skillet slipped when he tried to move it, and burned his little finger. Damn the woman.

Didn't she understand she couldn't be saying the things she did to a man? Or let him see her bare bosom, as if he could ignore those pretty little pink nipples? She couldn't be that innocent, no matter where she came from. Sam stared at the slab of bacon, black at the edges. Unless she wanted beans, she was gonna have to eat this. That's all there was to it.

He stroked the denim over his cock, willing the powerful need to go away. He'd been itching to bury himself in her softness all afternoon. If she kept up with her taunting, he couldn't guarantee he'd stay a gentleman. He ought to just tell her how he was feeling toward her. Be real plain about it so she'd understand what she was asking for when she let him see her bosom, and said those things.

"Sam? You burnin' something?"

At the sound of Doc's voice, Sam abruptly moved his hand away from his fly and stood to face his friend. Doc had shaved since this morning and wore fresh black trousers, and his coat looked as if it had been cleaned. He walked straight, as if he'd been off the whiskey for the better part of the day.

As he got closer, Doc sniffed the air. "Smells like burnt bacon."

"Yep."

"I reckon I'll be eating supper at the hotel," Doc said, grinning.

Sam snorted with false irritation. Truth be told, it did his heart good to see his old friend looking sober.

"Where's the woman?"

Sam gestured with a nod to the back, fighting the sudden image of round bare breasts with pink nipples. "Finishing her bath, I reckon."

Doc frowned at the pan of over-brown biscuits and then at the skillet. "You're not gonna feed her that swill."

"Yep. Being as it's her fault." He set his jaw, and then turned to stoke the fire when his friend's eyes got too curious.

"She ought to eat a proper meal," Doc said after a long stretch of silence.

Tempted as he was to remind Doc that he usually drank his supper, Sam kept his mouth shut. He glanced ruefully at the food. Wouldn't surprise him none if she wouldn't eat, and Doc was right. She'd worked hard last night, and no telling how much sleep she'd gotten. He finally shrugged. "I reckon I could go buy a chicken dinner at the hotel and bring it back."

"Hello, Doc."

Both men turned, and at the sight of her, Sam's heart skittered. She wasn't wearing a bonnet and her hair was damp, and her face pink from scrubbing. So was the skin at her throat, where she'd left the top two buttons of the brown blouse unfastened.

"Afternoon." Doc tipped his hat.

Sam took off his Stetson and slapped it against his thigh. "I've had mules less stubborn than you."

Her steps slowed and she frowned, her lips pursed in a pout. Just like she was fixing to kiss somebody. That didn't help his irritable disposition.

"Sam." Doc's disapproving tone wasn't welcome, either.

"You just come sauntering out here, without your bonnet, not knowing who I'm talking to. Seems to me you wanna get thrown in Sheriff Ames's jail."

She planted her hands on her hips and glared at him. "I recognized Doc's voice."

Sam grunted.

Doc stared at him with a look of complete shock. Then his mouth curved in a slow smile, as if he knew something Sam didn't.

"Come on, Sam." Reese walked toward him, a sway in her hips he didn't trust, and then she slipped an arm through his, real familiar like.

Well, he had seen her breasts. His insides tightened at the memory.

She smiled up at him. "What smells so good?"

*Her.*

He stiffened as he inhaled the clean, warm scent of her body. Staying close to this woman was dangerous. As politely as he could, he shied away from her and went to crouch down over the cooling skillet, poking at the black edges of the bacon. "I reckon we'll be eating a restaurant meal."

The fool followed him, bringing temptation with her. She peered into the pan, standing so close that her skirt brushed his arm. Even down here he could smell her pleasing scent.

"Actually, I love burned bacon. I don't eat it much, but when I do that's about the only way I have it. The fat gets cooked out so it's much healthier. But I have to admit, that bacon looks different than the kind I'm used to," she said thoughtfully.

Frowning, Sam glanced over at Doc, who seemed more interested in him than Reese's peculiarity.

Doc grinned suddenly. "No sense in you going to the hotel, Sam. I mean to go over there anyway." He backed toward the street, tipping his hat at Reese. "I'll see what Floyd and Daisy cooked up this afternoon, and bring something back."

"Don't trouble yourself," Sam said meaningfully while rising from his crouched position. "I'm headed that way."

"No trouble at all."

Sam clenched his jaw. He suspected he knew the reason for Doc's contrariness. But the matter was quickly settled with the loud bang of a gunshot. They all exchanged weary glances. The violence had begun early today.

SOMETIME AFTER NINE Reese finally was able to choke down one of the hard dry biscuits. The roll wasn't so bad dipped in coffee. Or maybe it was because she was so weak and famished she didn't care what anything tasted like. At first, Sam had told her to stay in the livery, since Doc was sober enough to take care of the wounded men who'd started parading into his office before the sun set. But as the casualty rate grew, Sam had reluctantly asked her to help.

She hadn't minded, except for the obvious risk factor. Fortunately, the men who came through Doc's doors weren't the law-abiding type who socialized with the sheriff. Observing how early medicine had evolved fascinated her. Some of it was hard to watch, though, because of the lack of sterilization, and Doc's limited resources to fight infections. Sadly, she guessed that one out of three men ultimately wouldn't survive.

Something else had happened during the course of the night that she hadn't yet had time to explore…a growing excitement simmering deep in her belly. Not over Sam, although her mind wandered to him far too much. Instead, she felt a renewed surge of wonder at the power of medicine, a feeling that she hadn't experienced since her second year of medical school.

"Things seem to have quieted down." Doc stood at the window, peering out between the parted curtains. Then he darted Reese a thoughtful look. "I have some beans in the back, and some dried beef."

Her stomach rumbled loudly, not that either offer sounded appetizing. She pressed a hand against her middle and murmured an apology. Without a word, Sam left the room.

Doc reached under the cot and pulled out a different bottle of whiskey than what he'd used for patients. He set two glasses on the small table where he kept instruments at hand, and glanced questioningly at her. She shook her head, disappointed in him.

He smiled knowingly, then poured himself half a glass. "You have a fine touch," he said, setting the bottle aside. He picked up the glass and cradled it in his trembling hands without taking a sip. "Sam doesn't understand, but I do need this to steady my nerves."

She smiled sadly but said nothing. The problem was, he wouldn't quit after the few sips it would take to stop the tremors. He knew that, judging by the way he quickly averted his gaze and downed a big gulp.

"Tell me what you did to the boy yesterday." He set the glass down, leaned against the wall and folded his hands together.

Yesterday? Had it only been yesterday that she and Ellie had been rummaging through Grandma Lily's attic? The idea was enough to make Reese dizzy, and she claimed the only stool. "It's called CPR."

Doc frowned, as she knew he would.

Feeling punchy, she couldn't help herself. "Or are you referring to when I performed the Heimlich maneuver?"

Looking baffled, Doc grabbed his glass again, and she instantly regretted baiting him.

Sam reentered the room carrying two cans, scowling when he saw the whiskey. His discouraged gaze moved to Reese. "The beans are cold," he said with a hint of apology.

"I don't care." At this point, she'd take protein any way she could get it. She watched him stick a spoon into the can, and when it looked as if he was going to pass the beans to her that way, she said, "But I'd like a plate if you have one."

Annoyance crossed Sam's face as he turned and left, but she guessed it wasn't directed at her.

Doc's chuckle confirmed her suspicion. "Sam's never been married. He forgets it's not a woman's habit to eat out of a can."

"I was wondering about that." She figured a man his age during this time period would have settled down and had a family by now. "Why hasn't he married?"

The good humor left the doctor's face, replaced by the haunted expression she'd seen there too many times in their short acquaintance. "You'll have to ask him. But I wouldn't be expecting an answer if I were you."

She smiled. "By the way, thanks for the clothes."

The abject bleakness that entered the man's eyes gripped her heart. God, how could she have been so thoughtless as to remind him of his wife's death? Reese knew from her experience during residency that it was best to acknowledge the loved one's passing rather than ignore the blunder.

She hesitated until she remembered his wife's name. "When did Martha pass away?" she asked softly.

He drained the whiskey from his glass. "Two years now."

"I'm so sorry."

He nodded, sighing heavily, his shoulders sagging as if the burden of his loss was heavier than he could bear.

"How did it happen?" she asked, testing the waters, seeing if he wanted to talk or would rather end the conversation.

During a brief but awkward lapse into silence, Sam returned. The tension was thick enough that he clearly picked up on it, somberly handing Reese the plate, his concerned gaze darting between her and his friend.

Finally Doc said, "Consumption took her. My Martha fought real hard." His voice cracked. "But in the end, I couldn't save her."

Reese scrambled mentally for the modern equivalent. Tuberculosis. How horrible that people died of something so easily curable. "It wasn't your fault, Doc," she said, fiercely shaking her head. "Even in my time, with all our modern knowledge, we have trouble saving people from consumption."

He stopped briefly, then reached for the whiskey bottle. He didn't appear surprised about her reference to being from the future, and Reese figured Sam had told him about her loony ranting. No, it was cautious hope that shadowed his eyes.

"I tried," he said despairingly. "I swear I wasn't drunk. I tried to save her."

She nodded sympathetically. "I've lost many patients to consumption myself, even after trying everything I knew."

A measure of relief eased the pain from his face. The tightness around his eyes and mouth relaxed, making him look considerably younger. However, her declaration didn't stop him from gripping the whiskey bottle and re-filling his glass.

Disappointed again, Reese looked at Sam.

His eyes met hers and his mouth curved in the faintest of smiles as he handed her the can of beans. She spooned some onto her plate, wishing with all her heart she could do more for Doc. How sad that he wasted his life by crawling into a bottle. The town needed him, and she had a feeling that, despite how it appeared at first glance, Sam did, too.

Doc ate a piece of dried beef—basically jerky, Reese decided—and then contented himself with his whiskey, while she and Sam ate the rest of the beef, beans and biscuits in melancholy silence. No gunshots disturbed them, and after a half hour, when Doc started nodding off, Sam suggested they return to the livery for the night. They both knew their sleep might be interrupted if more violence took place, but for now, they could close their eyes and forget for a while.

They said good-night to Doc, and then Sam checked to make sure no one was on the street before they stepped outside. Reese breathed in the crisp, clean air and gazed up at the clear sky. More stars than she'd ever seen at one time sparkled like pricey diamonds against the inky blackness.

Sam moved close and said, "Thank you."

"For what?"

He touched her cheek. "For lying to Doc."

# 9

IT TOOK JUST ABOUT everything Sam had in him to watch Reese disappear behind the door, and not follow her into the room. Touching her cheek had been a powerful mistake. Her skin was so damn soft it made a man want to break down and cry. He couldn't recall ever doing that. Not even when he was a tot. Had he shown that kind of weakness, he wouldn't be standing here now. But then, that might not be such a bad thing.

He threw another log on the fire and then got his bedroll out from where he'd tucked it behind the hay. No empty stalls were left after boarding Goliath, so he unrolled the bedding near the stove. He thought about forking some loose hay down from the loft for a cushion, but he was so tired even his teeth ached. Like last night, the hard ground wouldn't bother him.

Thinking about Reese was another matter. That could keep him tossing and turning. He wanted her. Against all good sense, he wanted her with a deep burning ache that had grown worse as the afternoon passed into night. He liked everything about her, including the way the devilment sparkled in her sassy green eyes. Mostly, he liked how kind and patient she was with Doc.

Sam suspected a lot of women wouldn't take kindly to a man who let spirits get the better of him. They didn't understand the demons some men faced. Him and Doc, they had more than their share breathing down the back of their necks. They'd seen too much senseless death, been responsible for some. That kind of guilt and shame stayed with a man no matter how much he drank or gambled or whored.

Some nights Sam got lucky. Like tonight, when his mind was too tired to fight sleep. He closed his eyes, breathed in deeply, but the peace wouldn't come. A vision of a green-eyed female stood in his way. What haunted him worse was the persistent feeling that he somehow knew her. Though he couldn't have met her before yesterday.

Before settling in Deadwood he'd drifted, living mostly on the trail, staying only a day or two when he passed through a town. On those rare occasions, Reese wasn't the type of woman he socialized with. She was too refined, cultured, a real lady.

Muttering a curse, he rolled over and tried to get comfortable, but even surrounded by straw, he could still smell her sweet tempting scent. No, he couldn't know her. He'd remember someone like Reese. For a lifetime...

He didn't know how long he'd been asleep when he heard the thundering of hooves. Sam quickly sat up as the horse galloped closer. It sounded as if the rider was headed to Doc's.

Sam scrambled to his feet and ran out of the livery just as young Pete Smith slid off his horse, his boot catching on the stirrup in his haste. Grounding out a string of oaths, he hopped on one foot before breaking free.

"Doc!" he hollered. "I need Doc."

Sam beat him to Doc's door, hoping like hell that his friend was still in good enough condition to handle this emergency.

"What's wrong, Pete?" Sam asked, using his shoulder when the door stuck.

"It's Sara. The baby ain't coming easy."

Sam finally pushed the door open and let Pete in. He was a young father, barely twenty, who'd already sired a son last year, and again his wife was with child. Sam hadn't known her name till now.

"Doc!" Both men called out at the same time. Except Sam didn't hold much hope that he would be answering.

They headed for the back room where he slept. His cot was empty. Sam led the way to his office. Just as he suspected, Doc sat on the stool, slumped against the wall, eyes closed, his glass lying on the floor. He'd passed out before he made it to his room.

"Goddamn it." Pete let out an anguished cry. "Sara's gonna die."

Sam pushed a hand through his hair. What could he do? It was one thing for Reese to hide out in Doc's office and help the drunks who would barely remember her the next day. But if she went to the Smith place and word got out…

Hell, he couldn't let the woman die. Fisting the front of Pete's shirt, he jerked him hard till the wildness in his dark eyes cleared. "I have someone who can help your wife."

Fear changed to hope in Pete's face. "Who? Let's get him."

"First, you have to give me your word that you will never speak of this night again. To anyone."

Pete nodded solemnly. "You have it. We gotta hurry."

Sam released him, told him to wait with his horse, and then headed for the livery. Pete's word would have to be good enough. Sam loosened his collar. It felt too much like a rope tightening around his neck.

AT THE SOUND OF the healthy baby's cry, Reese smiled through the exhaustion that minutes ago threatened to drown her. Tears wet her cheeks. Mainly from earlier frustration and fear that she wouldn't be able to help the young mother. But against all odds, mother and child were both doing fine.

Blond, freckled Sara, her hair and nightgown drenched with sweat, laughed through happy tears and cradled her son to her breasts. Reese kept her eye on Pete, who hovered unsteadily at his wife's side, one hand clutching the unfinished log bedpost, still looking as if he might faint. At the door, a toddler not much more than a year old stared absently into the small room. He hadn't once interfered, hadn't uttered a sound during his brother's long and difficult birth.

Sighing, Reese leaned against the wall and watched Sam quietly gather the soiled rags and bowls of bloody water. He'd barely left her side for the past four hours except to fetch and heat water, occasionally turning away to preserve Sara's modesty. Never once did he complain or balk when Reese barked an order at him. He stayed calm and purposeful.

"We have to leave," he said as he walked past her with the pile of rags. "Say your goodbyes."

"In a minute. I want to help sponge Sara down."

"No time." His gaze went to the threadbare curtains that covered the tiny window as he continued out the door.

She understood that he wanted to return to town while it was still dark, and she pushed herself away from the wall, amazed that her legs still worked. Reese was sure she'd been this tired before, during residency certainly, but couldn't remember it. The front of her blouse and skirt were totally ruined. She hadn't thought to bring an apron, only Doc's black leather bag, which he kept supplied for house calls. Pitiful, really, because most of the contents were ineffective.

"You and your baby will be fine, Sara," Reese said. "Later, try and eat something. Definitely hydrate."

The couple looked blankly at her.

"Drink lots of water."

"Thank you, Doctor." Sara started to cry again.

Reese promptly went to her side and covered her hand reassuringly. "You'll be fine. I promise."

The woman mutely nodded.

Reese didn't know what else to say. If she had to live in the middle of nowhere, in a two-room cabin in the woods, she'd cry, too.

"Doctor?"

She turned at the sound of Sam's voice, a tiny thrill skimming up her spine. She'd been called "Doctor" hundreds of times, thousands, but his acknowledgment pleased her in a way she couldn't describe.

"We need to go."

"Yes." She afforded Sara and Pete one last smile.

He released his wife's hand and straightened. "How much do we owe you?"

"Owe me? No." She shook her head. "Buy something for the baby."

Gratitude filled the young man's eyes. "Thanks, Doctor."

"Reese..." Sam's curt tone got her moving.

She wished she had time to clean up, but understood that returning to town after light would be risky. On her way out of the room, she grabbed Doc's bag and followed Sam to his horse. He climbed on Diablo first, took the bag and then held out a hand to her. As if she weighed nothing, he easily pulled her up to sit behind him on the saddle.

It took her a moment to arrange her skirt so that she could straddle the horse, and then she slid her arms around his waist and pressed her cheek to his strong, broad back. Along the horizon the darkness had already begun to fade. Hungry birds chirped in the trees. Sam clucked at Diablo and off they went, galloping down the dirt road through the woods. Reese held on tight, not just because they moved at a fast clip, but because Sam felt solid and safe and far more familiar than he should.

She truly wished they had time to stop, sit on a rise together, his arm wrapped around her as they watched the sun come up. But that could never happen, and that fact made her inexplicably sad. Silly, because she had far more important things to worry about. *After she slept,* she promised herself. If only for a couple of hours. She yawned and closed her eyes. Later, she'd worry about getting into the Golden Slipper. Later, she'd think about the small miracle she'd performed tonight, and how much it reminded her of the reason she'd studied medicine in the first place.

Right now, though, all she wanted to do was enjoy the feel of her breasts pressed to Sam's hard body, and the steady vibration of the galloping horse between her thighs.

TO REESE'S ABSOLUTE amazement, sleep hadn't come easily. Maybe it was because the sky had already turned pink by the time she'd fallen in an exhausted heap on Sam's cot. He'd been pretty certain that no one had seen them ride in the back way to the livery. Although some people in town had been awake. She'd noticed lanterns and candles lit behind window curtains.

Her rest was fragmented by erotic dreams of Sam lying gloriously naked beside her, before the image slid into a nightmare of him lying deadly still in a pine box. She gave up on sleep entirely after being awakened with the sensation of clawing an invisible wall, as if battling her way back to the future.

Despite her colleagues' predominant opinion that dreams

meant nothing, she believed the opposite. In her personal experience, dreams had often reflected her waking concerns, and when she took the time to think about them, they'd helped her solve problems. The dream about her and Sam lying naked together was a no-brainer. Yeah, she wanted him. She'd have to be totally numb not to be interested.

Painful as it was to replay the nightmare of him lying in the coffin, she knew her subconscious was trying to show her something she was too flustered to see. In the end, it occurred to her that the book with Sam's photograph could be the key to returning home. She'd held it in her hand just before she fell unconscious. Had she dropped it, or had the book traveled with her through time? Was it lying on the floor of the Golden Slipper?

The possibility had kept her wide-eyed and restless, until she'd finally sat up sometime around ten. Outside was still quiet, but she doubted Sam was asleep. She bent over to slip on her running shoes, and spied the books she'd noticed stacked under the cot. Unable to resist, she crouched down and grabbed a handful.

Behind the stack were a dozen or more books and magazines, which surprised her. Reese hadn't thought magazines existed in the 1800s. She pulled out several of those, too, and then sat down on the cot again, balancing the bounty on her lap.

She looked at the magazines first, stunned to find copies of the *Saturday Evening Post, Scientific American* and *Scribner's Monthly.* The issues were all old, even by Sam's standards, dating back three or four years. One publication, *Frank Leslie's Illustrated Newspaper,* particularly interested her. For the price of ten cents, the issue was filled with miscellaneous news in the areas of music, drama, fine arts, sports, serial fiction and book reviews. The pages were

# Get 2 Books FREE!

## Harlequin® Books,
### publisher of women's fiction,
### presents

# GET 2 BOOKS

We'd like to send you two *Harlequin® Blaze™* novels absolutely free. Accepting them puts you under no obligation to purchase any more books.

## HOW TO GET YOUR 2 FREE BOOKS AND TWO FREE GIFTS

1. Return the reply card today, and we'll send you two *Harlequin Blaze* novels, absolutely free! We'll even pay the postage!

2. Accepting free books places you under no obligation to buy anything, ever. Whatever you decide, the free books and gifts are yours to keep, free!

3. We hope that after receiving your free books you'll want to remain a subscriber, but the choice is yours—to continue or cancel, any time at all!

## EXTRA BONUS

**You'll also get two free mystery gifts! (worth about $10)**

# FREE!

**BUSINESS REPLY MAIL**

FIRST-CLASS MAIL    PERMIT NO. 717    BUFFALO, NY

POSTAGE WILL BE PAID BY ADDRESSEE

**Harlequin Reader Service**
**PO BOX 1867**
**BUFFALO NY 14240-9952**

NO POSTAGE
NECESSARY
IF MAILED
IN THE
UNITED STATES

well-worn, as if they'd been turned many times, although this particular issue was already six years old.

The thought of Sam being interested in this variety of subjects intrigued her. Eagerly, she turned her attention to the books, the jackets of which were already worn, and the first title leaped out at her: *Moby Dick.* Blinking, she went to the next one: *Nature,* by Ralph Waldo Emerson. Then two by Jules Verne, *Journey to the Center of the Earth* and *Twenty Thousand Leagues under the Sea.*

The familiar titles made her feel disoriented all over again. She checked the publishing dates. They ranged from the 1830s to the 1860s. She'd never thought about how long the classics had been around. But these books, right now, were part of Sam's pop culture. How interesting that he chose such fanciful fiction. Maybe that's why her fantastic story about traveling through time hadn't prompted him to throw her out.

She leafed through the pages, saw that some of them were dog-eared, and that a piece of straw or scrap of fabric marked a place. Tonight, if she couldn't sleep, at least she'd have reading material. She'd read *Moby Dick,* but none of the others. She set the books aside, and returned to the magazines. But a noise in the stables warned her that Sam was moving about, and she quickly put everything back under the cot.

She took a deep breath and smoothed her hair. Silly how her pulse sped up, knowing she was about to see him. But there it was.

"Did you want to be a doctor?" she asked after her first sip of morning coffee. Bitter and thick, the brew seemed to slither down her throat. But she needed to be alert, and this, if anything, would do the trick. Sitting by the heat of the wood stove was making her drowsy.

Sam stared down from the loft where he was forking hay to the stable floor. "No."

His appalled tone made her smile. "Why not? You're good at tending to people."

"Don't like blood."

She hooted with laughter. "You're kidding."

The annoyed dip of his eyebrows told her he didn't share the joke.

"But you're around gore so much. You're the first to hold down a patient or clean up or replace the bloody water—"

He winced. "Don't much like talking about it, either."

She drew her head back, surprised by his obvious aversion to blood. Then she took another thoughtful sip of coffee. He helped because Doc needed him, because without his contribution, someone could die. Had she ever met a more honorable man? Certainly not in her circles.

Damn him. As if she didn't like him too much already.

She shifted so that she could lean comfortably against the sideboard where he kept the pot, skillet and kettle, and watched him work. No hardship there. He had strong, muscled arms and seemed to handle his chores without effort. She knew guys from the gym who kept in great shape, working out religiously, yet she doubted any of them would have half his stamina.

"What did you do before you came here and opened the livery?" she asked.

He stopped forking hay, leaned on the pitchfork and used the back of his arm to wipe his forehead. He looked at her directly for the first time since she'd joined him, his gaze briefly lingering on her throat, where she'd left the top two buttons unfastened. "You shouldn't be sitting out here in the open."

"We'll hear if someone comes."

"Not necessarily."

She sighed. "After last night, I don't see that it matters. The Smiths probably have told someone about me."

"No. Pete gave me his word."

Reese smiled wanly, sincerely hoping that was good enough. Sadly, in her world, a person's word didn't always mean much. "You haven't told me about what you did before coming to Deadwood."

He stiffened, the tension radiating from his body reaching her half a floor below. Abruptly, he picked up the pitchfork and aimed it like a spear high in the air in her direction. Her heart plummeted. With force, the pitchfork pierced one of the bales of hay sitting several feet from her.

He pulled off one glove and then the other, stuck them in his back pocket. Then he descended the rickety-looking ladder, his brown shirt straining across his back muscles.

"You could have hit me with that thing," she said, her heart still pounding.

"Only if I'd aimed for you."

She glared at him. "What are you going to do now?"

He stepped off the last rung and turned to face her. "Water the horses, ma'am. If that's all right with you."

His teasing smirk caught her off guard. She gathered her skirt and pushed clumsily to her feet. He closed a hand around her upper arm to help steady her. When it was time to release her, he did so with such obvious reluctance that something fluttered in her chest.

She looked into his chocolate-brown eyes, tempted to slide her arms around his neck and hold tight until he kissed her. It would take but a second for him to respond. She hadn't mistaken the heated looks, the different ways he found to touch her, no matter how briefly. But she knew darn well they wouldn't stop at one kiss, and there was too much at stake.

"Why won't you tell me about your past?" she asked, tilting her head to look up at him.

His face changed, the humor gone. "What good is that?"

She lifted a shoulder. "You know about me. All I really know about you is that you like to read. You have quite an eclectic collection of books and magazines."

He startled her by hooking a finger under her chin and forcing it higher. His gaze skewered her with a contempt she didn't understand. "Do I?"

"The books were in plain sight. I wasn't snooping."

One side of his mouth lifted in a mocking smile. His grip on her chin tightened infinitesimally, just enough that panic welled up inside her. "What else did you find?"

"Nothing. I swear."

"I offered you shelter. That's all." His eyes were cold. This was the other Sam—the one she'd glimpsed yesterday.

She shivered. "I understand."

Abruptly, he lowered his hand.

She swallowed, even more curious about him than before. Surely he wasn't embarrassed at being well-read. Not that she'd ask.

Wordlessly, he refilled the cup he'd left on the stove. He took two gulps and stared out toward the street.

She had little choice. At the risk of getting her head bitten off, or worse, she asked, "Will you go to the Golden Slipper for me today?"

A muscle in his jaw jumped. Without looking at her, he gave a curt nod and drained his coffee cup.

There was only one reason a man went to a place like the Golden Slipper, and it galled her to think she cared in the least what Sam did. But her hand shook as she reached into her skirt pocket and withdrew the coins the patients had given her last night. She opened her palm. "You'll probably need these."

# 10

SAM STEPPED INTO the dimly lit parlor of the Golden Slipper. The sickening smell of tobacco, whiskey and cheap sex burned his nostrils and sat heavy in his lungs. He'd chosen a good time to come. The place was crowded, even though most of the miners had headed back up the mountain. Not long ago, when Deadwood had first sprung up out of nothing, the whole town depended on gold and prospectors for survival. But that had changed quickly, with folks pouring in and setting up shops and saloons. Now with talk of the railroad, and the telephone exchange with Lead, it seemed as if there were never any peaceful days.

The stage came more often now, the livery was nearly always full, and what with Homer Atkins opening another hotel, Sam had been asked to add to the stables. He didn't mind the extra work, but he hated the steady increase in travelers coming through town. It was only a matter of time before someone recognized him.

"Well, I'll be. Sam Keegan. I haven't seen you here in quite a spell." Margaret sidled up to him, her strong perfume making his eyes water. "You haven't been going over to Dora or Mollie's place, have you, darlin'? My girls are much better than those old whores of Dora's. Those gals of hers have been spreading their legs before mine were born."

He waited for her to finish laughing at her own joke, and then said, "No, ma'am. Been too busy."

She linked an arm with his, and with her blue satin skirt rustling, steered him toward the bar. "Chester," she said to the barrel-chested bartender. "You give Sam here a whiskey on the house."

"Thank you, ma'am," Sam said, even though pressed up against Margaret's big bosom and drinking a whiskey was the last thing on earth he wanted.

She drew a finger across the seam of his lips. "You call me Margaret, handsome." She smiled, her taunting gaze following the trail of her finger, and then she slowly lowered her hand. "I have the perfect girl for you, Sam Keegan. You just wait right here."

He exhaled slowly and watched her sashay toward the stairs. Damn, he wished he could've slipped in without her seeing him. Truth be told, the fact that she knew his name surprised him. He didn't even really know the woman, who'd come to Deadwood about a year ago. Her establishment was the newest of the three brothels. Sam had only visited the place twice. She and the sheriff had gotten real cozy right off, and Sam made it a habit to stay away from lawmen.

Chester set the whiskey in front of him, and Sam nodded to the man before throwing back the shot. He hadn't wanted it, but no use having people wonder why a man would belly up to a bar and not take a drink. The bartender picked up his glass to refill it, but Sam shook his head and slid him a coin, which he quickly pocketed.

"Heard you had some excitement around here on Saturday," Sam said in a tone that meant he was just making idle talk.

"Saturday?" Chester frowned, shaking his head, his

fleshy jowls wobbling. Abruptly, his face cleared. "Oh, Saturday, yeah, the new whore. Wearing a wedding dress, if you can believe it. Then gone, just like that." He snapped his fingers.

"They found her yet?"

"Nope. Why?"

Sam shrugged. "I like 'em with spirit. Figured I'd have a go at her."

Chester grinned. "Yep. That one, she had spirit." He wiped his hands on his apron while he glanced around. Then he ducked his head and gulped down a shot from a glass hidden under the bar. He straightened and looked around again, his pale blue eyes darting toward the stairs. "A man can get mighty thirsty working back here. But Margaret don't understand."

"Good thing she's not here." Sam smiled, reaching into his pocket. Not the one that held the coins Reese had given him. Hell. Big of her, offering to buy him sex. That had really set him off. "Let me buy you another one."

The bartender's greedy gaze went to the gold piece Sam set on the bar. He narrowed his eyes on Sam, paused for a second and then grabbed the gold. "Don't mind if I do."

Sam waited for the man to down another shot, and then said, "The woman, the one in the wedding dress. Did she leave anything behind?"

Chester gave him an odd look. A customer at the end of the bar yelled for another beer and the bartender shifted his girth in that direction.

Cursing under his breath, Sam looked around the room. A bald man he recognized but didn't know by name sat on a settee with two of the ladies. Already he'd had too much to drink, judging by his crooked tie and the fact that his pocket watch had fallen on the floor near his boot. The blonde hanging on his left arm slid a hand between the man's legs, and smiled at Sam.

He quickly turned back to the bar. The last thing he needed was to have to fight an angry drunk. He waited for Chester to refill glasses, hoping he'd get done before Margaret returned. Finally, the man ambled back in his direction.

"I'll take another whiskey now," Sam said, so as not to arouse suspicion.

Chester grumbled about washing another glass, and then shoved the whiskey across the bar. Sam got his meaning and gave him an extra two bits.

"Margaret said she had someone in mind for me." Sam sipped, and then shrugged. "You got an opinion on who I should choose?"

The bartender's lecherous gaze went straight for the blonde who'd smiled at Sam. "Any man who goes up those stairs with Laura comes down grinnin' from ear to ear."

Sam briefly glanced over his shoulder and then took another sip. "Sure had my mind set on the new one."

Chester pulled the towel he kept draped around the back of his neck and polished a wet spot on the mahogany bar. "Don't know what to tell you, friend."

"You expect she means to come back? Did she leave anything here she'd wanna fetch?"

"Nope." He stopped and frowned thoughtfully. "Come to think of it, she didn't have any bags with her."

"Nothing?"

"Not a damn thing." Chester snorted. "Must have been expecting Margaret to buy her a wardrobe. Ask me, Margaret's better off without her." He shook his head. "Some of them whores from back East, they're just more trouble than they're worth."

Sam nodded in mock agreement, glad he had some time

to think when the man went to refill another glass. Reese had come with nothing, which suited the story she told of traveling from another time. Hard to believe as it was, pieces of the puzzle fit together like nothing else did. Trouble was, if she hadn't brought anything with her, what the hell was he supposed to be looking for?

Whatever it was, it plainly wasn't to be found. She'd left nothing behind, and he knew for a fact this place had always been the Golden Slipper, from the time it was nothing but a few sticks in the ground.

He saw Margaret at the top of the stairs, trailed by a tall, big-bosomed redhead. Sam swore to himself at the same time the thought flashed in his mind that he might do well to get some relief. He started growing hard just thinking about the softness of Reese's golden skin, how her hips curved just like a woman's ought to. But Margaret's whore was a little young for his tastes. She barely looked eighteen.

She also wasn't Reese. The unexpected notion shook him all the way down to his boots. The woman was gonna be the death of him. He gulped down the rest of his whiskey and pushed back from the bar.

Lucky for him, two men stopped Margaret and the redhead at the foot of the stairs. The interruption granted him enough time to leave without causing a ruckus. Chester was at the end of the bar, and on his way to the door, acting on a sudden impulse, Sam asked, "What's Margaret's last name?"

Chester eyed him as if he'd had one too many whiskeys. "Winslow," he said. "Margaret Winslow."

SHE SHOULDN'T HAVE SENT him to the Golden Slipper. It had been a mistake. A huge mistake. Reese paced the length of the livery, stopping to pat Diablo's velvety nose, taking a deep calming breath and hoping to dispel some of the nervous energy that had her so keyed up she couldn't keep still. As she'd done every five minutes for the past hour, she edged her way to the entrance of the livery, and cautiously poked her head out far enough to check for any sign of Sam.

Nothing.

She should have found a way to sneak into the Golden Slipper and look for the book herself. If he found it, he'd probably look at it. He liked books. He'd be curious. And then he'd see his own picture, of him dead, propped up in a pine box. Oh, God. She couldn't imagine his horror. What had she been thinking?

Well, she *hadn't* been thinking. That was part of the problem. Her mind was a muddled mess, bouncing from one thought to the next. She needed sleep and a decent meal. And what she wouldn't give for a real bath.

However, none of those comforts would help determine one vital decision she faced. If suddenly given the magic key, could she leave, knowing Sam was destined to hang? Could she return to the future and not torture herself over his fate? What happened now, or next week for that matter, was already history, she'd tried to reason with herself.

The possibility also existed that he deserved to hang. He'd frightened her twice now. Right before her eyes she'd seen him change from a soft-spoken, thoughtful man to one who seemed as if he'd just as soon spit on her than help her to her feet. So why wasn't she still frightened of him? Why did her heart thud with sick panic over his safety?

Maybe she'd been brought here to save him. The thought had occurred to her more than once. If she didn't fight the reality of actually being here, then perhaps she needed to consider the reason for her circumstances. Except giving in to lunacy wasn't that easy.

Shaking her head, she resumed pacing and noted the stiffness in her neck. What was keeping him so long? Stupid question. The Golden Slipper was a brothel, after all. And Sam was a man. He'd think nothing of sampling the wares. The mores were different here. The fact that it made her jealous was laughable. No, it was disgust, not jealousy, she told herself. Yet she'd given him the money to pay for the sex.

She groaned loudly, startling the horses.

There should be only one objective in her mind: getting back to the twenty-first century, where a lucrative career awaited her. Abruptly, the idea of being made up for a live broadcast sent an arrow of distaste straight through her middle.

Her memory flashed to Sara Smith's slick, beaming face as she held her newborn baby. Reese had enjoyed her work in the past couple of days. She'd literally saved lives. Even residency hadn't compared to the hands-on gratification of bringing someone back from death's door. But she'd have that same opportunity later on…in L.A. In a big, clean, modern hospital with all the latest technology. Twice a month she'd collect a nice fat paycheck. Nothing wrong with wanting it all.

She thought about Doc's dirty office and that pathetic shelf of castor oil and heaven only knew what else. Her stomach lurched. Even small changes could improve the survival rate of his patients. Still, there wasn't much she could do but make suggestions and explain to him about CPR and the Heimlich maneuver and pray that he'd stay sober enough to retain the knowledge. It wasn't as if she could forget her other life in another time and stay here. That wasn't possible. The mere idea knotted her insides. Another idea registered. Would the decision even be hers?

She pressed a shaky hand to her stomach and forced herself to breathe deeply, trying to rein in her thoughts, trying to keep from getting ahead of herself.

Right now her goal was simple. She wanted Sam back. Here. Safe. With her.

DOC'S HAND SHOOK SO BADLY he had to drop his blade into the basin of sudsy water or risk slitting his own throat. He angled his face to look at the reflection of his jaw. The stubble poked out worse most days, although he'd wanted to look respectable for Reese. She'd done real good helping bring Sara Smith's baby into the world, and he aimed to buy her a restaurant-cooked supper. That is, if he could make himself look her in the eye.

Shame and guilt bathed his skin in sweat. A deep yearning for the bottle he'd hidden under some rocks behind his office almost made him howl like an injured wolf. But he wouldn't touch it. Not today. He wanted to keep a clear head and learn what he could from Reese. She knew things about healing he'd never heard of, and she hadn't lost a single patient. Sam had described her outrageous claim about being from the future. Doc wanted to hear more. He wanted to discover her medical secrets. It's what Martha would have wished.

Just thinking about his wife stoked the urge to uncover the bottle and drown his misery. He clenched his teeth and wiped the sweat from his brow. Later. If he still wanted a drink after he talked to Reese, then so be it. For now, he could do this. Not take a drink. If only for an hour or two.

He abandoned the razor and splashed his face with the cooling water. Things would be better if he shaved; a face without whiskers always made him feel like a new man. But he could only take one small step at a time. Might be that if he got some food in his belly, his hands wouldn't shake so bad.

He dried his face and hands, pulled down his cuffs and buttoned them, and then slipped on his coat and set his hat on top of his head. Too late he recalled he hadn't combed his hair. It needed cuttin' and tomorrow, God willin', he'd go to the barber. Right now it was enough for him to put one foot in front of the other.

Halfway across Main Street, he saw Sam coming from town, his strides long and quick, his face as dark as a thundercloud. Doc waited for him, wondering if his friend's sour disposition had anything to do with a certain blond doctor of the fairer sex. He tried not to smile. Even with a head as big as a water trough and his mouth drier than a cotton ball, he knew better than to goad Sam when he was in a black mood.

Doc waited at the entrance to the livery. Out of the corner of his eye, he thought he saw movement near the stove. Likely it was Reese, no doubt wearing one of Martha's dresses. Swallowing hard, he forced his thoughts away from the image. Martha would have been glad to share her clothes. She would've done anything for the woman.

God, he wished she was here. Sharing his bed. Pressing a cool damp cloth to his forehead when the nightmares came. Martha had known everything about his past, and even when he'd forsaken himself, she'd loved him anyway.

"Sara Smith had her baby last night," Sam said by way of greeting. "A boy."

"I heard." Doc nodded and walked with him into the livery. Sam stopped, frowning. "Who told you?"

"Pete was in earlier looking for some castor oil."

"He say anything about Reese?"

"Not a word."

Relief relaxed Sam's features. Neither of them doubted Pete understood speaking in front of Doc was all right, but still, it had been a good test.

"He did say that Sara hadn't had an easy time of it," Doc murmured, fresh shame washing over him. "Her mama had the same problem. The fifth child killed her. Hope Sara and Pete are more sensible about having too big a brood."

Sam's dark gaze searched the back of the livery. "You seen her?"

"Not yet. Where've you been?"

"The Golden Slipper."

Doc stared in disbelief. "What the hell for?"

The corners of Sam's mouth twitched as he headed toward the stove and stooped to get the coffeepot. "Reckon I don't have to explain that to you, Doc."

"And here I suspected you were sweet on the lady doctor."

Sam's head jerked up, his eyes narrowing dangerously. He shot a look toward the back before fixing Doc with a menacing glare.

Chuckling, he held up a placating hand. "Now, I'm certain she's sweet on you, so why you'd find the need to go to the Golden Slipper—"

"She sent me."

Doc's amusement abruptly fled. "She sent you?"

"Yep," Sam assured him, with a smugness that made no sense.

The door to the back room creaked, claiming both their attention as Reese walked out. She gave them each a quick look and blushed.

Doc cleared his throat. Hell, he hadn't meant for her to overhear. "Afternoon, Reese."

"Hello, Doc." Her anxious gaze went to Sam.

"You didn't leave anything behind," he informed her, his gaze on the coffee he poured into a cup and passed to Doc.

"How do you know?" She moved toward them, wearing Martha's favorite blue blouse with the eyelet trim around the collar.

Doc stared into his murky black coffee, willing the pain and resentment away. Wouldn't do any good to fault Reese for being here when Martha couldn't be.

"I asked the bartender."

"Maybe he doesn't know. Maybe one of the women picked up something—"

"Chester knows everything that goes on there."

She heaved a shaky sigh and clasped her hands together. "Did you find out anything useful?"

"Nope." Sam poured Reese a cup, his focus on his chore. He was holding something back. Doc wasn't sure what was going on, but he'd known Sam for nearly half his life. He spoke as plainly as any man Doc had ever met. Not now.

"You were gone a long time," Reese said, with a dose of accusation in her tone. She quickly glanced down at the cup Sam had handed her, her fingers wrapped around it so tight her knuckles looked white. "Never mind."

Doc sipped his coffee to hide his smile, then, to break the awkward silence, said, "I reckon you're trying to get your belongings back from the Golden Slipper."

She looked at Sam. "Apparently, I traveled light."

"I told Doc." Sam scrubbed at his face. He looked tired, and Doc felt renewed shame over being out cold last night when young Sara needed him. "About where you say you're from."

"I figured." She met Doc's eyes. "I know it sounds crazy. Sometimes I don't believe it myself. But if there's another explanation for me suddenly appearing here out of thin air, I'd love to hear it."

Doc considered the earnestness in her lovely green eyes. He sincerely hoped she wasn't out of her head. She just might be the woman who could pull Sam from the pit of hell. He needed goodness and sunshine in his life, and a week ago, Doc would've sworn on Martha's grave that there wasn't a woman on God's green earth that Sam would allow himself to feel anything toward. But these past two days Doc had seen a spark in his friend's eyes that had never been there before.

"You know, I believe our last conversation got interrupted. I'd still like to hear about what you did for the boy the other day," he said, and offered her his arm. "How about I buy you a nice steak supper at the hotel?"

Her startled gaze darted to Sam. "I'd love to discuss medicine with you but—"

"Don't be a fool," Sam interjected. "She's not going anywhere."

She gaped at him, her eyes blazing.

"I thought you told the sheriff she's a friend of mine," Doc said, all innocence. "No harm having a quick supper."

"The hell you say." Sam dumped out his coffee. "The woman is staying here."

Reese's hands went to her hips. "*The woman* will make up her own mind."

Doc watched the two of them eye each other like wildcats in heat, and gleefully sipped his coffee again, suddenly not missing his whiskey at all. Now that he'd stirred the pot, no telling what would come to a boil.

# 11

DEEP DOWN Reese knew Sam was trying to protect her. Protect him and Doc, too, because if she got caught, the sheriff would want to know who'd been hiding her. Not that she'd ever breathe a word, but she understood where Sam was coming from. What she wasn't willing to accept was that he thought he could lord it over her.

"You know what?" She held his challenging gaze and took a couple of steps toward him to make sure he knew she wasn't afraid of him and that she meant business. "It might be the custom here to tell a woman what to do, but in my time it doesn't fly."

He frowned, and too late she realized it might also be a custom to slap a mouthy woman. But she wouldn't back down. Not now that she'd drawn her line in the sand. Besides, she felt safe with Doc here.

But Sam didn't look angry. Confused, maybe. Probably wasn't used to a woman talking back to him. Doc, on the other hand, looked as if he was enjoying himself a tad too much.

"Lucky for you," she continued, "I intend to be reasonable." She shook her head at Doc. "I wouldn't be comfortable out in public. But thank you for your offer."

Doc smiled. "Sam might have a point. Better we don't have to answer any questions. I can bring some food back. I reckon you're tired of Sam's cooking by now."

"Honestly, neither of us has had time to cook or eat," she said, and noticed Doc flush a dull red. She certainly hadn't meant to remind him of his neglect. "You look good today, Doc," she added softly, and reached over to squeeze his big rough hand. "I hope tonight isn't too busy. We can have a nice chat."

"Monday night. Should be slow."

"Good." She included Sam in her smile, and then tried to keep any hint of the ridiculous jealousy she felt out of her voice when she asked, "Do you have any money left from the Golden Slipper for our supper?"

Wordlessly, he reached into his pocket and pulled out a handful of coins and a couple of gold pieces. She didn't know the exact amount she'd given him, but he couldn't have used much, if any. The relief she felt was silly. Made not a bit of sense. If he wanted to screw every woman in town, it was none of her business. Nor did she care. Maybe it would improve his disposition.

Her gaze lingered on his large, callused palm, and she wondered about what kind of lover Sam would be. Was he generous? Or did he take what he wanted, quickly, without thought of pleasing his partner? Annoyed at the direction of her thoughts, she snapped her gaze to Doc.

"I don't know what things cost, but will that be enough for all of us?" She refused to look at Sam, even though she felt his troubled eyes burn a hole right through her.

Doc chuckled. "Yes, indeed. But I'm buying. I suspect you should keep that in a safe place in case you need passage."

Reese sighed as she watched Doc walk toward the street. He still didn't believe that she belonged in the future. If he did, he would understand that she didn't need passage. She wasn't going anywhere, unless it was through some weird time vortex. What about Sam? If he didn't believe her, either, had he done his best to find evidence at the Golden Slipper?

She turned to discover him watching her, his brooding expression totally unnerving. "Do you believe what I told you about where I'm from?"

"Yes." He said the word quietly and without hesitation.

"What changed your mind?"

"Margaret," he said, "from the Golden Slipper. Her last name is also Winslow."

Her heart thumped wildly in her chest. "Margaret? Scary Margaret?" Reese decided she needed to sit down. "Damn."

Sam's dark eyebrows shot up.

She vaguely registered that he wasn't accustomed to a woman using such language, and then took the only stool near the stove, her thoughts racing so fast she felt dizzy. On the bright side, the news helped validate her claim. But why did it have to be Margaret? The woman gave her the creeps.

"Why didn't you tell me right away?" Reese asked, watching him throw another log onto the fire.

Crouching, he used a poker to stir the ashes and reposition the wood. "Reckon I should have."

That hardly answered the question, but there was little use pushing him. She stared at his strong, stubborn profile. He was a very attractive man. Obviously well-read. Why did he tie himself to this place, practically living like a hermit? She knew from Doc that Sam hadn't been married but, had he, like Doc, lost someone he deeply cared about? Had the loss made him bitter? "Did you speak to Margaret?" she asked.

"No point to it."

She stared down at the thick black goop coating the bottom of her cup, and murmured, "No, I guess not."

Okay, now what? At least she hadn't imagined that the

Golden Slipper looked like Grandma Lily's house. As disgusting as the thought was, Margaret most likely was Reese's grandmother with four or five greats in front, or possibly a distant great-aunt who'd bequeathed the home to her brother. Reese liked that possibility much better and was sticking to it.

"So?"

She looked over at him.

He lowered himself to the floor and sat with one long leg bent at the knee, bracing an arm. "What do you reckon you'll do?"

"I don't know. Try to sneak into the Golden Slipper."

His face darkened and he jabbed the poker into the logs with too much force.

"It's not like I want to go anywhere near the place, but the house is the only link I have to home." She switched her attention to the fire and stared at the hypnotic flames. "Don't worry, I won't ask for any more help from you."

"I'm not complaining."

"I know." She realized with sudden clarity that she couldn't get him involved. Not with the threat of a noose in his future. It amazed her that she could be so self-absorbed that she sometimes forgot what Sam was about to face.

She had to warn him. Now that he finally believed she lived in another time, she could explain about the book, about seeing his picture. Caution him to stay away from Goliath and his owner. The man would leave with his horse soon enough. The danger would pass. History would be rewritten.

Gathering her skirt so she wouldn't trip, she scooted the stool closer to Sam.

He narrowed his eyes in suspicion when she reached for his free hand. As soon as she touched him, he tensed, holding himself so absurdly rigid it might have been funny under any other circumstances. She splayed her much smaller hand over the back of his, squeezing gently.

Maybe the contact hadn't been a good idea. She'd only meant to help cushion her words, but oddly, the innocent touch sent a shaft of heat all the way to her belly. Pulling away now, though, would make everything worse. "Sam, I have something else to tell you. It won't be easy to hear."

He didn't say anything, didn't move, didn't even blink.

"First of all, I know you're a good, honorable man."

He jerked back, and with a harsh laugh said, "Don't make that mistake."

"Sam, please."

He rose. "I have chores to do."

"Just give me a moment."

"The horses can't wait."

"I'll help." She struggled to her feet, tugging at the folds of the skirt when they tangled around her legs.

"You." He didn't offer assistance, but spun toward her with a finger jabbing the air. "Stay out of sight."

"I can't very well do that for the rest of my life, can I?" She heard his sharp intake of breath, and then watched him stalk toward the steps to the loft, his pounding footfalls sending dust and grit into the air.

She had a good mind to follow him up to the loft. At least there she could corner him. Make him listen. What the hell was wrong with him? He acted as if she'd insulted him, which clearly wasn't the case. Did it somehow show weakness to be considered a good man?

He grabbed the pitchfork and quickly ascended the steps. As soon as he disappeared from sight, hay came flying down toward the stalls with a vengeance.

"Fine," she said, not really prepared to carry out her

bluff, but he'd annoyed her. "I can talk from here. All you have to do is listen."

Silence fell.

Then the pitchfork came spearing through the air, fortunately landing nowhere near her this time. He climbed down, and her pulse quickened, watching the play of worn denim across his perfect ass.

"You're trouble, lady," he muttered, sending her a scornful look as he walked past her toward the first stall. "Too damn much trouble."

The distinctive saddle he picked up from the railing she recognized as the one from last night. He took it into Diablo's stall, and the gelding tossed his head in anticipation as Sam started to saddle him.

She growled with frustration when she understood he was leaving. "Where are you going?"

Mutely, he finished fastening the straps and then swung into the saddle.

"Doc is bringing back dinner," he muttered.

At the click of Sam's tongue, Diablo surged forward. "Stay out of sight," he warned again, and then trotted out of the livery, angling left, away from town.

DINNER HAD BEEN a simple meal of roast beef, fried potatoes and canned corn. Not the kind of food Reese normally ate, but she cleaned her plate and still had room for apple cobbler. Sam's plate remained untouched, sitting by the stove, covered with a white cloth napkin. Doc stayed sober, sipping coffee and asking her dozens of questions about CPR, the Heimlich maneuver, methods for sterilization and treatments for common ailments.

She enjoyed appeasing his unwavering curiosity, knowing that he vacillated between outright disbelief and

cautious astonishment. For hours no emergencies interrupted them. Not even Sam. She'd been anxious, wondering what he could possibly be doing away from town in the
dark, and voiced her concern several times. But Doc
seemed frustratingly unperturbed, and she had to satisfy
herself that he considered Sam's behavior normal.

At nine, barely able to keep her eyes open, she stifled a
yawn. Doc promptly excused himself, first making certain
she was safe behind the door to the back room, and reassuring her that Sam would return soon. She left her clothes
on and lay back on the cot, staring into the dark.

Ten minutes ago she'd been so tired she'd feared falling
asleep on Doc. Restless now, she thought about lighting a
lantern and reading one of Sam's books, but decided that
keeping the place dark might precipitate his return. She
hoped that would happen soon. Every little sound made her
edgy in the unfamiliar blackness. Sam had been here the
last two nights, and even though he was still basically a
stranger to her, she felt oddly safe when he was around.

Perhaps her complacency was foolish. After all, history
described him as a criminal, and she'd seen that harsh side
to him twice now. But neither mattered. Instinctively, she
trusted him, and he hadn't let her down yet. He'd even
found out that the Golden Slipper belonged to a Winslow.

The idea still boggled her mind. She didn't know of
anyone in her family who'd explored the Winslow ge-
nealogy. Or if they had, they'd kept the information about
Margaret quiet. Reese smiled. Wouldn't sharing that tidbit
at cocktail parties be a hoot?

That is, if she could find her way back. Her amusement
faded. Would there be any more cocktail parties to attend?
Any more invitations to sit on televised panels? Spa treatments? Leisurely laps in her pool? She shifted on the

narrow cot, lifting herself up on her elbows because it was suddenly difficult to breathe.

With the smell of hay and horses heavy in the air, her Beverly Hills life suddenly seemed so faraway it was almost nonexistent. What if she wasn't meant to return? What if this was it for the rest of her life? No, she couldn't allow those thoughts. She'd only been here three days, barely enough time to find the key that would take her back home. She closed her eyes and forced herself to breathe deeply and evenly.

But what if this *was* it?

She shivered, trying with all her might to shove away the persistent question. Staying here wasn't an option. She had important work to do. Modern medicine was on the verge of so many previously elusive cures, and she desperately wanted to be a part of it all. She'd worked hard to be included, to help make a difference. Yes, the hands-on work of the past two nights had been enormously satisfying, but meant little in the scheme of her life's plans.

A noise outside made her bolt upright. The steady rhythm of trotting hooves came from beyond the warped door, the sound somewhat distant, as if the horse and rider were still on the street. She held her breath, listening to the whinny of the horses, apparently alert to the newcomer.

The fall of the hooves grew louder and she knew the rider had entered the livery. It had to be Sam. Right? But it didn't, of course. The person could be a customer. Or the sheriff. She stayed totally still, clenching her teeth and listening.

She thought she heard the rasp of saddle leather, then a soft light entered the room past the ill-fitting door. A dozen possible threats flitted through her mind before she was calmed by Sam's low, rumbling voice as he talked to the horses.

Unclenching her teeth, she breathed with relief. Only briefly did she consider opening the door, and then she lowered herself back down, adjusted the makeshift pillow under her head and closed her eyes. She was so tired and now she could sleep. She felt safe. Sam was back.

HE TRIED NOT TO MAKE too much noise. The last thing he needed was her yappin' at him. But the horses had gotten excited, Diablo had hurt his left hind leg and it took Sam a few minutes to get everyone settled down. He eyed the door, hoping like hell she was on the other side. The notion that Doc could've gotten drunk instead of bringing back her dinner had bothered Sam some. Left on her own, the hardheaded woman was likely to have gone poking around the Golden Slipper and jeopardized herself.

Sam cursed under his breath. She was something, all right. But he wasn't obliged to keep her out of jail or away from a whore's life. He appreciated what she did to help Doc, but there was a limit to how much a man could take. And Sam couldn't bear her thinking he was something he wasn't.

Since sunset the air had cooled down more than usual. He stirred the ashes in the stove and threw on another log before laying out his bedroll. His belly growled when he saw the covered plate of food. Three hours had passed since he'd eaten a piece of dried beef.

The warmth from the stove had kept the meat and potatoes from getting too cold, and he sat with the plate on his lap and ate steadily until only the corn remained. That was something he didn't much care for, but it wasn't his habit to waste food, so he forced down most of the yellow kernels before washing his plate and fork.

She thought he was a good man. Damn crazy woman. Where the hell had she gotten such a faulty notion? She didn't know him. Didn't know the evil he'd done. Against his will, his mind kept going back to the earnestness in her shining green eyes before he'd left. Hell. Her wanting him to be good didn't make it so. Never would. He'd killed and maimed, and nothing could change the past.

Over the years the images and sounds had dimmed a touch. Some days, especially when he was busy helping Doc, Sam could almost forget about the kind of animal he was. The wails in the night lessened, as did the image of blood and guts exploding across the forever changed landscape. The fading of memories had been his only saving grace. He didn't need her forcing him to relive what he couldn't undo.

Feeling guilty about riding Diablo so hard, Sam checked on him before pulling off his boots and putting out the lantern. Then he hunkered down in his bedroll and did something he never did, even though God didn't want to hear from the likes of him. He prayed. For all he was worth, Sam prayed for numbing sleep.

*Black smoke rose above the collapsed buildings and the burned and mangled corpses littering the street. The air was so thick Sam couldn't catch his breath. With all the smothering smoke he couldn't see Jake. Where was his friend? He'd been standing beside him a moment ago. Was he dead?*

*Sam's hand closed tightly around the butt of his rifle as fear choked the last of the air from his lungs. He tried to call out for Jake, but then gagged and sputtered until the sickness rolling in his belly forced its way up to his throat. He bent over and retched. After he'd emptied his belly, he retched again.*

*Behind him someone pleaded for mercy. Sam spun around. An older, portly man, bloodied and broken, lay in the street with an outstretched hand. Spittle caked the corners of his mouth, and his thinning hair was plastered to his forehead by the same blood and sweat that stained his nightshirt.*

*No one knew the gang was riding in. They'd surprised the town in the middle of the night. The townsmen hadn't had time to arm themselves. The women peeked out from behind pretty curtains, their eyes wide with shock. By now the screaming and wailing and gunfire had mostly died down, but the ugly sounds still echoed in his head.*

*Sam's vision blurred and he blinked, swiping at his eyes. His face was wet. His gaze flew to his hands, checking for blood. He stared down at his damp, colorless fingers. And then furiously wiped at the tears on his cheeks before the other men witnessed the humiliation.*

*"Please," the man on the ground whispered, his voice reedy as he stared up with defeat in his eyes. "If you have any decency left—"*

*Angry, Sam glared at him and raised his rifle, aiming the barrel at the man's head. He'd seen Sam's tears. The bastard thought him weak. But who had the gun? Who had the power in his hands?*

*The man sighed, his bleak eyes drifting closed as he drew in his arm, a small, grateful smile quivering at the corners of his bloody mouth.*

*Sam's gut tightened. He lowered the rifle, staring feverishly, his whole body beginning to tremble. The man wasn't asking to be saved. He knew he wouldn't survive, and wanted to be spared a long painful death.*

*He wanted Sam to kill him.*

*Sam couldn't move. Couldn't breathe. Could scarcely look at the man's twisted body. The putrid smell of death burned his nostrils, took the starch out of his knees. Desperate panic gripped his insides until he thought he'd retch again.*

*Goddamn it. Where was Jake? They had to get out of here. Run as far as their legs would carry them. Before Captain Quantrill and the rest of the men knew they'd gone. This wasn't about the war anymore....*

*"Son?"*

*Sam looked back down at the man, the pallor of death already having staked its claim.*

*"Please, son," the man begged. "Show mercy."*

*Sam blinked back the threat of new tears, and slowly raised his rifle. He aimed at the spot right between the man's eyes. And pulled the trigger.*

# 12

REESE AWOKE with a start. She sat up and stared into the darkness. It was still night. No early morning sunlight seeped into the room. So what had awakened her? Had there been a noise?

As the fuzziness of sleep started to clear from her brain, she thought she heard something. She stayed still and quiet, her ears straining toward the door. An anguished groan had her throwing off the handmade quilt and finding the hard floor. Without the help of a lantern, she fumbled for the knob and then used all her strength to pull the stubborn door open.

The livery was dark but for a soft orange glow coming from the stove. She took a tentative step, and seeing movement, froze. The large heap near the fire moved again. She breathed with relief when she realized it was Sam. Was that where he slept since he'd given her his cot? Had he made that awful noise?

Her answer came in a strangled cry that made her skin crawl. He must have woken himself, for he abruptly sat up, his head turning in her direction.

"What's wrong?" he asked.

"I don't know. I heard a noise…You must have been having a nightmare."

He hung his head and exhaled loudly.

"Are you all right?" She moved closer.

"Go back to bed," he said without looking up.

"What's wrong, Sam?"

He didn't answer.

"Was it a nightmare?"

"Leave." He ground out the single word in a harsh voice that should have sent her scurrying back to the room.

Instead, she crouched beside him and put a soothing hand on his forearm. His skin was hot and clammy, and he snatched his arm away.

She got back up and went to the room for a washrag, which she dipped into the bowl of water sitting on the three-legged stool. When she returned, he looked up at her and muttered a curse. Ignoring him, she lowered herself and sat back on her haunches. With the cool damp cloth, she stroked the back of his feverish neck.

He jerked at her touch and grabbed her wrist, his hand tightening painfully. The dying fire cast ominous shadows across his face, distorting his features. "I don't want you here."

She swallowed around the lump that had lodged in her throat. "Tough."

He glared at her for nearly a minute before abruptly releasing her.

Reese resisted the urge to rub the skin around her wrist. It smarted from his punishing grip, and she wouldn't be surprised if she found bruises later. Tentatively, she returned the cloth to the back of his neck, mentally prepared for another outburst. But he only heaved a sigh of disgust and shook his head.

She let the silence stretch and then asked, "Is this where you've been sleeping the past two nights?"

He gave a curt nod.

She winced at her own selfishness, having given no

thought to whether he'd had another bed. "I'm sorry for taking your cot. I'll sleep out here from now on."

He didn't quite smile, but cocked an amused eyebrow at her.

"What? You don't think I'm capable of roughing it?" Taking advantage of his softening mood, she moved the cloth to his forehead.

Scowling, he ducked his head. "Enough."

She glared. "Who's the doctor here?"

"I'm not sick."

"Please, Sam, don't push me away. I still don't know what I did earlier that made you mad."

He kicked away the bedroll. "You want coffee?"

"I want us to talk."

He got to his feet with a show of temper. "Christ almighty, woman, don't you know when to keep your mouth shut?"

"No." She scrambled up after him.

He stood facing her, but the tension radiating from his body warned her of his simmering fury. She should have been frightened, and she was a little, although if she kept backing down he'd keep pushing her away.

He took a step toward her. "I know one method to shut you up."

She lifted her chin. "Really?"

He made a sound of exasperation before grabbing her upper arms and roughly pulling her to him. He hesitated, as if giving her a chance to ward him off, and when she ignored it, he lowered his head and claimed her mouth.

The kiss wasn't gentle. He angled his head and pressed hard against her lips, forcing past the seam with a hard thrust of his tongue. Obviously he was trying to frighten her, but achieved the opposite effect. She slid her arms around his neck and kissed him back, her tongue dueling with his, the sudden yearning for his touch burning deep in her belly. Her breasts ached with it, and the temptation to draw him back to the small room and strip him bare fueled an enthusiasm that caught her off guard.

He released her arms, and she briefly thought he might push her away. But he caught her at the waist, and then one hand slid around to the small of her back, urging her closer. She sighed into his mouth, and he pulled her even closer, until their bodies touched and her breasts were crushed against his muscled chest. She felt the buckle of his belt dig in just above her waist, while the hard length of his penis taunted her.

Heat surged through her body, so intense it was as if molten lava coursed through her veins. She craved the feel of his work-roughened hands on her sensitive breasts. She desperately wanted to stroke the silky steel of his shaft. When he ran his hand over the swell of her backside, she moved her hips against his erection.

He groaned, the guttural sound coming from deep in his throat. His plundering tongue turned so forceful she stumbled backward. He held her upright, slowing the kiss, and then abruptly released her. He moved back, breathing raggedly.

"Had enough?" he asked hoarsely.

"Not nearly." She clutched his arm when it looked as if he was about to walk away. "Sam, please."

"Go back to the room," he ordered and she watched him turn away to adjust his fly. "Close the door. I won't bother you."

She half laughed, half sobbed. "Don't you get it? I want you to bother me."

He shook her arm free and went to stoke the dying fire. A flame licked up, illuminating the tortured expression on his face. "I'm not the man you think I am," he said quietly. "Now go."

"I know enough to respect and admire you."

He let out a coarse laugh.

"I know that I want to do more than kiss you. I want to see you naked. I want you to touch my breasts."

He jerked a look toward her, his eyes gleaming with baffled fascination.

She crouched beside him and laid a hand on his arm. "If that shocks you, I'm sorry. Women in the future are different than what you're used to. We're equal to men in every way, and we're not considered whores for wanting the same things men want. In bed or out."

He didn't look convinced as he turned back to tending the fire.

"We have the same needs, and we aren't ashamed to voice them. Sometimes we even tell a man what feels good and what we'd like him to do to us."

The look of horror that crossed his face made her press her lips together to keep from laughing. "Sounds a mite dangerous," he muttered.

"No, actually, it works out quite well for all parties."

He gave her another sharp look, his gaze narrowing, probing. Maybe he thought she was teasing him. "Tell me what you like."

She blinked, taken aback by his sudden interest. "Well," she said, hedging, until she noticed the smirk tugging at his mouth. So he was calling her bluff? That was all the incentive she needed. "Let's see…." She stared at the flames. "I like long slow kisses, lots of cuddling. I like my neck kissed right here." She pointed to the spot below her ear, and then met his eyes. "Oh, and I like my nipples lightly bitten and my breasts suckled kind of hard."

The smirk vanished from his face. He dropped the poker, got to his feet and wiped his palms on his Levi's. Standing directly in front of her, he couldn't hide the growing thickness behind his fly.

"I'm not done," she said.

"You try a man's patience."

"Oops. Sorry. Didn't mean to." She grinned, and pushed herself up.

He helped her to a standing position, then tugged her hand, forcing her to take a step closer. "I've killed men. Many men," he said flatly.

She sucked in a breath. His statement shouldn't have shocked her, but it did a little. Though this was a different time, people played by different rules... Sometimes they had to kill to survive. "I'm sure you had good reasons."

"Some of those men didn't even need killing." His face was hard, his voice emotionless.

She swallowed convulsively. "You don't carry a gun," she said lamely.

"The deeds were done long ago. Not carrying a gun now doesn't change who I am." One side of his mouth hiked up. "Still think I'm a good man?"

Her mouth was so dry she couldn't speak. She could only stare at him, unwilling to believe the picture he tried to paint. Why was he doing this? Was he that eager to be rid of her?

Sam released her hand and hooked a finger under her chin, forcing it up. He waited until he'd captured her gaze, his eyes mocking, and then stroked the back of his fingers down her cheek. "You still want me to do those things to you?

She moistened her lips and slowly nodded. "Yes."

First surprise, and then pain flickered in his face. He hastily withdrew his hand as if the touch had seared his skin. "Get out of here before I change my mind," he whispered through gritted teeth, and turned sharply away.

"No."

Slowly, he faced her again. "You don't know what you're saying."

Reese started unfastening her blouse. "Bring a lantern," she said, briefly meeting his watchful eyes, and then headed for the room.

Her heart raced with the enormity of what she was doing. How could she trust this man after what he'd just told her? She was by no means a stupid person. Not only did she have a high IQ, but she had the good fortune to possess common sense. After Sam's admission, there wasn't a single logical reason why she shouldn't run and hide. Stay as far away from him as possible. Yes, she'd seen how admirably he'd assisted Doc, experienced his kindness firsthand, but she'd also witnessed that streak of hardness that hinted at his capacity for violence.

So why did every instinct tell her that she wasn't wrong about Sam? He was a good man, in spite of what he claimed. He had no reason to lie, and every reason to hide the ugly truth. There was more to his story, she was certain of it. She wanted to hear it, too. But not now. She had other plans for him.

She undid the last button and shrugged out of the cotton blouse, shivering not so much from the cool air as from the idea that Sam would be joining her. That is, she hoped he would, and hadn't gotten back on his horse and taken off again.

She glanced over her shoulder, suddenly uncertain. A light flickered, and she breathed with relief because he'd lit the lantern. She turned around to face the doorway while she unsnapped her skirt and stepped out of it. A moment later Sam appeared, his hair damp around his face, and she briefly lamented not having used the washbowl herself.

He carried the lantern into the room, his gaze staying on her as he set the light on the chest. "Last chance," he said reluctantly.

She smiled in answer and reached around to unhook her bra. She let it fall away from her body, snatching it up before it hit the ground.

Sam's lips parted slightly, desire burning so hot in his eyes that she felt a little light-headed. While he watched her, she cupped the weight of each breast and played with her already beaded nipples.

She heard his sharp intake of breath, and then he yanked the shirt from the waistband of his Levi's. The garment didn't have buttons going all the way down like modern ones. The buttons stopped midway, and he only unfastened the top two before pulling the shirt over his head and flinging it toward the door.

He had two scars, one near his right nipple, and the other a remnant from an older injury, a long, thin white line below his rib cage. His chest was well muscled, with just a smattering of hair, and his belly enviably flat. He undid his belt, pulled it free and dropped it where he stood. His boots were not so easily removed, and she smiled at his impatience as he jerked each one off with a grunt.

She quickly got rid of her own shoes, but left on the panties. Sam unsnapped his Levi's, watching her with an intensity that could be warning or desire, she wasn't sure which. She shivered and went to him, seeking his warmth. His hands stilled in the act of removing his jeans. She put her palms on his broad chest and then slid them up until her arms were looped around his neck and her bare breasts flattened against the hard muscle.

They both shuddered. He stroked his hands down her back, his palms rough and callused but surprisingly gentle. He cupped her bottom and drew her firmly against his erection. She moved her hips, just a little, just enough to show him she planned on full participation. He groaned quietly, and then, demonstrating what a good student he was, lowered his head and nuzzled the spot near her ear that she'd showed him.

She smiled at the slight tickle from his stubble and let her head loll back to offer her throat. His hot mouth glided over her skin, the damp heat from his tongue leaving its mark as he made his way to her collarbone.

"You're so…beautiful," he murmured, his warm, moist breath dancing across her sensitive flesh.

Reese brought her head up, and he abruptly claimed her mouth, his tongue immediately exploring. She kissed him back, hard and sure, leaving no doubt what she wanted. When his hand found her left breast, she arched into his palm, her craving for his touch driving her a bit mad. He lightly pinched her nipple, rolling the nub between his thumb and forefinger, as if testing the texture, before splaying his palm and cradling the full weight of her breast.

She wanted to see him, all of him, but she didn't want him to stop the light, torturous kneading. Lowering her arms, she reached between them and finished unfastening his Levi's. When he realized what she was doing, he moved back, giving her enough room to pull the denim down his hips.

His long underwear went down with his jeans, his hard and ready cock sprang forth, making her pulse race out of control. She paused in her mission, and then finished dragging the underwear and denim down his thighs, brushing the hard, silky tip with her lips as she forced the Levi's to his ankles.

Sam sucked in a startled breath. Quickly, he rid himself of his clothes. Before he could take further action, she guided him to the cot and urged him to sit. His dark eyebrows dipped in confusion, and she kissed his forehead right there where the two drew together. He was so much taller than her, she'd already planned her strategy.

She stood between his spread thighs, plunging her fingers through his thick dark hair for balance while he slipped the red silk thong down her legs. It still amazed her how gentle he was, so much more than she'd expected. With one steadying hand at her waist, he held the panties for her to step out of.

He didn't immediately cast the thong aside, but stopped to briefly study it with a bewildered look on his face.

She smiled. "Bet you never saw anything like that before."

He slowly shook his head, and with far more reverence than he'd handled the other clothes, he set the scrap of silk beside him on the cot.

Reese laughed, the sound quickly dying when he took a nipple into his mouth. With a hand molded to each side of her waist, he ran his palms over the curve of her hips and then back up while his tongue flicked and rolled around her nipple. After a couple of repetitions, and giving her other nipple its due, he moved his hands to her breasts, pushing them together so that he could get both nipples in his mouth, suckling them so greedily that she could barely stand.

He must have felt her slight swaying, for he looked up at her, his eyes glazed, his lips damp. "I want you," he said hoarsely. "I want to be inside you."

She nodded numbly and let him urge her backward.

He got up, and she couldn't stop staring at the sheer beauty of his smooth thick shaft, the crown already glistening with moisture. He lifted her chin and kissed her, his lips warm and firm against hers, and then he pulled the quilt to the foot of the cot. Her panties disappeared in the folds, and she had the crazy thought that she'd have to remember where to find them.

It almost felt as if she was standing behind a one-way glass, watching a movie scene being set. He rearranged the straw pillow, and then smoothed out the thin sheet covering the cot. She had no idea what he was planning. She doubted the cot could support their weight. Not that she cared. He could spread the sheet on the bare floor and she'd gladly follow him down.

He moved out of a shadow, and her breath caught when she saw the ugly, flat round scar near his right shoulder blade. A burn had left that mark. Almost as if someone had branded him. Was that how he'd paid for his sins? She didn't want to think about his past right now. Or his future. At the reminder of the photograph of him propped up in the coffin, she shuddered.

He turned to her, his dark eyes troubled and probing. "I won't force you."

"No." She gave him a tight smile. "I know. It's not that." She had to tell him what she knew. Just not right now. She put out her hand.

He took it, his hungry gaze running down her body before he hauled her up against him. He cupped her bottom and held her steady while he moved his lean hips. Her breath caught at the amount of heat his cock seemed to give off. She reached between them and wrapped her palm and fingers around his hot, swelling flesh. He pulsed in her hand, his breath hissing between his teeth.

Taking her by the shoulders, he led her cautiously backward until she felt the edge of the cot behind her legs. She understood his intention and lay down, looking up at him. He truly was a striking man in every way, from his intense brown eyes to the glistening manhood that inspired a hunger in her she'd never experienced before. She wouldn't be patient much longer. If he didn't—

He grabbed her calves just above the ankle and pushed her legs until they bent at the knee. She wasn't shy about her body, but when he sat on the cot before her, she wasn't quick to let her knees spread. He did it for her, prying her legs apart, his obvious impatience making him a little less gentle than he'd been before.

His eyes briefly met hers before his gaze homed in on the juncture of her thighs. He forced them farther apart, his nostrils flaring at what he saw. His gaze unwavering, he kissed the inside of one knee.

And then he put a finger inside her.

# 13

REESE JUMPED at the invasion. She thought she'd been ready, but he'd surprised her. His hand stilled as he watched her, uncertainty in his eyes.

"It's okay," she whispered.

He didn't seem convinced, and since she didn't know what else to say, she thrust forward so that his finger went deeper. She closed her eyes at the delicious feel of him, moaning when he hit just the right spot. Her reaction apparently gave him confidence and he spread her nether lips, his eyes drinking their fill, before he circled the small nub and had her arching off the cot.

Slowly he withdrew his finger. "You're not a virgin." It was more a question than a statement, an odd dread in his tone.

She blinked, and held back a laugh. "No. It's different in the future. Few women my age haven't experimented sexually to some degree."

He looked relieved. "You're still tight."

She did laugh then. "I haven't exactly screwed an entire fleet."

He frowned, and she caught on that he wouldn't understand the word *fleet*. And then he touched her again, with just the right amount of pressure, bringing exquisite pleasure to her every nerve ending, and proving some things were timeless. With his free hand, he cupped her left breast and then, using the pad of his thumb, teased her nipple with a circular motion.

She didn't know why, because she wanted him as much as he wanted her, maybe more, but she automatically clamped her thighs together. A ghost of a smile touched the corners of his mouth and he turned his hand, silently asking for better access. She immediately parted for him, and with his eyes still on her face, he kissed the inside of her bent knee.

Her need to feel him inside of her intensifying, Reese almost told him he could skip the taking it slow part, but she liked all of this, too. She liked the tender way this big strong man gazed at her, touched her as if she were a breakable porcelain doll. She hadn't expected this treatment, although that was stupid, because she hadn't really expected anything.

He'd told her he was a killer. That should have been enough to strike fear in her heart. But there was more to it. There had to be. She had good instincts about people. Besides, Sam had nightmares. He might have killed someone, but he had a conscience, he felt regret.

She moved her head so that she could see his hard, thick erection, but before she could touch him, he groaned, grabbed her ankles and straightened her legs. She let out a small shriek of surprise but he caught her mouth with his, silencing her, as he threw one leg over the cot and straddled her.

Her breasts heaved with excitement, nudging his chest, the warm, crisp hair there tickling, exciting her even more. He trailed his lips to her nipple, nibbling lightly, first one and then the other. His rigid sex lay hot on her belly, and she shifted with impatience.

He stopped to look at her, his gaze somber, his biceps trembling with restraint. "I don't have any— I don't want to make you pregnant," he said in a husky voice.

"You don't have to worry about that. It's taken care of."

He frowned slightly, his gaze going to her mouth.

"Another modern miracle." She wasn't about to explain about advances in birth control at this point. Instead, she lifted her hips so that she rubbed the base of his cock, and watched as his restraint shattered.

The gentleness disappeared from his face, and she didn't mind at all when Sam roughly pried her thighs far enough apart to allow him entry. He guided himself to the soft folds, probing until the broad head of his penis gained a stronghold. His eyes closed briefly, his neck corded with his clear attempt at control. His hard, muscular thighs kept hers spread, and even if she'd wanted to she couldn't stop the slow hot penetration.

Trying to ease the coiling tension low in her belly, she clutched his muscled shoulders, her nails digging into his skin. But he didn't seem to notice. He pushed in another inch and then gazed down at her through dazed eyes before squeezing in a little more. He was trying to let her get used to him, she realized with a sudden giddiness.

Reassuring him that the fit was perfect, she rocked her hips, clenching her muscles around him as he pushed into her. He needed no more encouragement. He thrust back, so deep, so hard that a cry breached her lips before she could stifle it. She moved with him to let him know it was okay, and to get him to ignore the uncontrollable tears seeping from her eyes down to her hairline.

With his head thrown back, his shoulder muscles bunching, his body gleaming, he looked savage as he pumped into her with a steady forceful rhythm that pulled her to the brink of mindlessness. She reached down to touch herself, but he slid his hand beneath hers and unerringly found the pleasure spot. He'd barely begun to work his magic when the first spasm hit. It shocked Reese, and her whole body convulsed with the intensity.

Relentlessly, the waves came, until she had to bite her hand to keep from screaming and waking half the town. He came at the same time, his pounding rhythm turning frenzied when she met his every thrust. He moaned loudly, and then arched his back with a final plunge that left them both trembling.

He withdrew slowly, his glazed eyes finding hers, his hands molding her breasts before smoothing down the side of her ribs and over her hips. He almost smiled, but then leaned back and pushed away from her. She started to protest, until she recognized it had to be uncomfortable for him on the narrow cot.

She watched, praying he wouldn't simply walk out of the room. When it looked as if that's exactly what he planned on doing, she lifted herself on one elbow. "Sam?"

He picked up his Levi's and looked at her.

"Don't go."

He shifted uneasily. "You need sleep."

"So do you. We'll sleep together."

He scrubbed at his face. His Levi's blocked the important stuff, but he had a damn fine chest, and she felt another tingle of arousal.

She slipped off the cot before he used it as the obvious argument for not staying. Although the way his gaze slid down her nude body, as if he could devour her in seconds, she figured he might be too single-minded to think that far ahead. But she wasn't taking any chances.

She slid her arms around his waist, went up on tiptoe and let the friction of her sensitive breasts against his chest do the convincing. He lowered his head, and she pressed her lips to his, opening for him when he probed her mouth with his tongue. She kept the kiss short, though, and then said, "I'll be right back."

"Reese." His scandalized voice stopped her before she'd even touched the doorknob.

"I'll be right back," she repeated. "I promise." And then she yanked open the door, shivering because it was cooler out in the open livery.

The fire was almost dead, most of the light gone, but she found the bedroll. She should have known. Before she managed to grab a decent hold, he was there beside her, draping the handmade quilt over her shoulders.

She smiled, though he doubted he could tell in the darkness. "I wouldn't have come out here if I thought anyone would see me."

"Go back inside."

She started to protest, but then saw him crouch down and roll up the bedding. Sighing, she led the way back. For goodness sakes, she should have just asked him to get it in the first place. She was so used to doing what needed to be done herself.

He dropped the bedroll on the floor, and she shoved the door shut, wishing it had a lock on it. She let the quilt fall from her shoulders, draped it over her arm and turned back to Sam. He stared at her as if he had no idea what to do next.

HE'D NEVER BEDDED A LADY before. When a man got done with a whore, he left. He didn't make idle talk, or lie with her beyond the act of coupling. He sure as hell didn't sleep next to her. But Reese wanted him to stay. Might be that was one of the differences between a whore and a lady. Bold as she was, Reese was still the latter. From her petal-soft skin to the sweet scent of her hair.

Just looking at her perfect pale breasts, he started getting hard again. If he stayed in this room, they wouldn't sleep. That was one thing he was sure of.

"Sun's coming up soon," he said. "Reckon I should go tend the horses."

"No." She tossed the quilt on the cot and went to him. "The sun won't be up for a couple of hours." She slid her arms around his waist and pressed her cheek tightly against his chest. In his hand, the thick denim of his Levi's stood between them, separating their bodies. If she felt his hardened cock, she might reconsider. He tossed the Levi's aside.

She shivered and moved snugly against him, allowing his erection to nudge her belly. His arms automatically went around her.

"You sleep on the cot," he said, his throat so dry he didn't recognize his own voice.

"No." She pulled away and glanced at his bedroll. "There's room for both of us."

"The ground is hard."

She shot a look at his manhood, opened her mouth to say something, and then just smiled. She sat on the bedroll by crossing her ankles and gracefully lowering herself. As her knees opened, his breath caught at the sight of her. The soft blond curls hid most of her secrets, but he knew what was there, and that was enough for sweat to break out on his brow.

"I forgot the quilt," she said, her gaze going to his midsection.

His cock twitched. He grabbed the coverlet and lowered himself beside her as she stretched out. If she thought he could keep his hands off her, she was sorely mistaken. Lying on his side, he braced his head with one hand, and with the other, traced the line where the skin around her nipples met the golden tone of her belly.

"Sun has touched you here," he said, lightly dragging his fingers over the velvety softness. He didn't understand how she could remain so soft after having been marked like this. The sun made his own skin rough and leathery. Who could have forced this on her? Why? "What happened?"

She glanced down and smiled. "Nothing happened. In my time it's considered attractive to be tanned. Not too much, or it's bad for your skin, but lots of men and women like to have a little—" She gasped when he rolled his thumb over her nipple.

He smiled in turn, and put his mouth on her. She closed her eyes as he suckled her, relaxing back against the bedroll. He wished he could take her to the hotel. She deserved a proper bed. But the risk was too great.

He hadn't seen her move, but he jerked at the feel of her small hand wrapping around his cock. She started at the base and knew just how much pressure to use as she stroked up to the tip. Surprised at how hard and ready he was, he leaned back, fighting for control over his body. She used the space he gave her to pump him slowly until the pressure was too great to ignore.

*Ah, hell.* He'd told himself he'd go slow this time. His restraint slipping, he urged her to turn on her side, and quickly entered her from behind. She was ready for him, hot and slick and tighter than a glove. He closed his eyes and sank deeper into her, regretful that his mouth couldn't catch her sweet whimper.

She moved against him, her smooth firm buttocks rubbing his belly as she drove him to madness. He curled an arm around her slim waist and cupped one of her taut round breasts. It took only moments for him to explode. He groaned loudly as he emptied his seed into her, with so much fierceness that he shuddered violently.

She had to be a witch. No woman had ever made him feel like this before.

She quivered in his arms and slumped against him. He couldn't stop touching her tight budded nipple. She moved her head, and he kissed the side of her neck as he slipped out of her. She made a soft mewing sound and wiggled her buttocks into the crook of his thighs, as if seeking comfort he didn't know how to provide.

"Good night, Sam," she whispered, laying her arm over his, tugging it more snugly around her.

He tensed, not sure what to do, or if he wanted to stay here like this. But she was so delicate and supple in the circle of his arms, her sweet feminine scent pulling at him until his brain was too muddled to form a sensible thought. Inhaling deeply, he relaxed, and felt the gentle rise and fall of her bare bosom against his arm.

His chest tightened in an unfamiliar way. Here she was, snuggled up to him, bare as the day she was born, and strangely, it wasn't desire that stirred in his loins. The sudden protectiveness he felt toward her shocked him. He had no experience with the feeling. Sure, he'd been looking out for Doc and all, for some time, too, but this was different.

Was this what being married felt like? He'd never given thought to it before. That he had now sent an uneasy feeling through his gut. He wasn't the marrying kind, and even if he was, no decent woman would have him. He could never provide a wife with a respectable life. For him, survival meant sticking to the shadows, forgoing the town picnics and dances and all the polite socials a woman needed.

He listened to Reese's quiet, even breathing, unsettled that she'd fallen asleep in his arms. With a dawning amazement, he realized she trusted him. She trusted that she'd be safe, that he'd protect her.

That he wouldn't hurt her.

Warmth flooded his chest, and for a second he didn't think he could breathe. Other than Doc and Jake, had anyone ever trusted him so completely? Panic gripped him. He shifted so that they weren't so close. The little fool thought he was a good man. She couldn't be more wrong.

She was like silk, and willing, and she'd given him much-needed relief, but he'd be the bigger fool if he reckoned she could mean anything more than that. Bad enough that since she'd come the nightmares had returned, after months of quiet sleep. She caused them to return, he thought with sudden clarity. All her crazy talk about him being a good man.

His thoughts went to Jake, to that black day when everything had gone to hell. Satan himself had come to call that night in Lawrence, Kansas, and Sam had traded his soul, not knowing it was for the promise of eternal damnation. He should've been the one to die. Not all those innocent men who'd had the bad fortune to possess what Captain William C. Quantrill coveted. But Sam had been a coward.

Reese sighed in her sleep, squirming until her buttocks were once again flush against his privates. The temptation to take what she offered held him frozen for another minute. And then he came to his senses, and slowly moved far enough back that he could roll over without disturbing her.

He got to his feet and found his Levi's, drawers and shirt. He didn't dare stop to get dressed, but quietly carried his clothes out of the room. Once he was on the other side of the door, he inhaled deeply. Today he'd help her get the hell out of here. And then maybe the nightmares would stop again.

REESE FLOPPED ONTO her back and rubbed her sore hip. As bad as the cot was, the hard ground had been miserable.

Sam was gone, which didn't surprise her, because the sun was already up. She yawned and stretched, and then pulled the quilt up to her chin. She was tired enough to sleep another few hours, but she didn't dare. Especially not lying here naked like this, with only that sad excuse for a door between her and whoever happened by the livery. But then again, maybe she could tempt Sam into crawling back under the quilt with her.

Her belly and breasts got tingly as she thought about last night. She never would've guessed he could be so tender. A couple of times he'd lost it and got a tad rough, but not enough to frighten her. And he hadn't been at all selfish. In fact, in the few relationships she'd had, she couldn't remember feeling more sated. He knew just how much pressure to use, just how deep to kiss her, as if they'd been perfecting their play for years. It was kind of scary, mostly because she felt she knew Sam better than she really did.

She thought she heard something, and listened for a moment. It was Sam, she was pretty sure, feeding the wood stove. Slowly, she raised herself to a sitting position, surprised at the aches that had nothing to do with the hard ground. Had it been that long since she'd been with a man? She remembered it had been quite a while. Medical school and her residency rotation hadn't afforded much opportunity to nurture a relationship.

Besides, she hadn't met anyone interesting in a long time. Certainly no one like Sam. And, gee, she only had to travel a hundred thirty years back in time to meet him. She squeezed her eyes shut at the reminder. She had to get back home. And once she did, she'd never see Sam again.

Her eyes flew open and the air seemed to whoosh from her lungs like a punctured balloon. Her hand shook as she threw back the quilt and got up. Why this reaction, she didn't know, because that wasn't new information. Sam lived here, now. She lived in the future. That wasn't going to change.

But had she? No, of course not. Panic edged close to reason. The intimacy they'd shared was interfering with her logic. She had responsibilities, family, work obligations. Her decisions involved far more than just herself. She totally understood that.

Damn it. How could she have been so stupid as to make love with him?

So, it was simply afterglow, she told herself, as she sorted through Martha's blouses. Reese found a dark blue one made of light wool, a little too thick for the warmth of the afternoon, but she'd be going braless today. Had she been thinking clearly last night, she would've washed her underwear before she went to bed, so it would be dry by now.

But obviously, she hadn't given much thought to anything. Yes, the sex had been great. The best she'd ever had. But that's all it was. Sex. A haven of comfort in the swirl of uncertainty. She'd felt safe in Sam's arms, protected. But nothing had changed between them. Nothing could.

She slipped on the blouse and buttoned it before splashing her face with water Sam had left in the bowl. After she was done, she divided the remaining water between the bowl and the basin and added soap flakes to the former. Then she scrubbed her bra and panties until her knuckles were as red as the expensive silk. Never again would she take her washing machine for granted, she thought as she rinsed her things in the basin. She didn't know how people here had enough time to do everything.

The selection of skirts was slim. Thinking longingly about her huge walk-in closet full of designer clothes, Reese winced and settled on a skirt that was a shade darker blue than the blouse. A hideous match to be sure, but she wouldn't get anywhere being picky.

She had a lot to do today. She'd promised Doc she would review some of the procedures she'd described to him, so that he could write them down. She pulled on the skirt and sat at the edge of the cot to slip on her shoes. Belatedly, she noted she should have washed her socks, too. Ladies' stockings would be easier, so maybe she'd ask Sam to pick up a pair at the general store.

The idea of asking him to do something so personal for her brought her up short. She was just being silly, and that wasn't like her at all. She stood, adjusted the skirt and ran her fingers through her hair. She moved to the door and hesitated, surprised that she was nervous about seeing Sam. In that moment, through the wooden panel, she heard Hastings Barnett announce himself.

# 14

"GOOD MORNIN' TO YOU, Mr. Keegan," Hastings Barnett said in his distinct East Coast accent. "I've come to collect Goliath."

Listening at the door, Reese felt her heart beat wildly. If the man left Deadwood, the threat to Sam would be gone. At least that line of thinking seemed reasonable. Not that there'd been any logic to the past three days.

"He's a fine animal," Sam replied. "Looks as if he's got some Arabian."

"Perhaps. I won him in a game of draw poker from a Texas rancher." Hastings Barnett laughed. "Lucky for me, those boys down South like their cards and whiskey. Ever been to Texas, Mr. Keegan?"

"I spent some time there," Sam said slowly, almost reluctantly. "I'll add up your bill."

She fisted her hands to keep from trembling. She wanted Barnett gone. Now. Back to wherever it was he came from. As long as he was faraway from Sam.

"Happy to pay up, Keegan, but you misunderstand. I have business at the mine today. I'm bringing Goliath back this afternoon."

Reese groaned with despair. She clamped a hand over her mouth, but it was too late, judging by the men's abrupt silence. They made no more small talk, and soon she heard Goliath trotting out of the livery, obviously carrying his owner. Even when she thought it must be safe to leave the room she waited for Sam's knock, which seemed to take forever.

She pulled the door open, stunned at the sudden wave of shyness that swept over her when she saw him. He wore his usual Levi's and a tan shirt, and his long, dark, wavy hair was the same. Still, today he looked different. Taller. Broader. More heart-stoppingly handsome.

"Hi," she said, her voice barely audible. She cleared her throat and tried again. "Good morning."

He nodded, his gaze flickering to her breasts.

The thickness of the wool fabric didn't seem to matter. Her puckered nipples strained against the blouse, making it obvious she wore no bra. "I had to wash my underwear," she murmured.

"There's coffee and biscuits," he said brusquely, looking away. "Doc came looking for you."

"Does he have a patient?"

"Nope. Said you were gonna meet up with him today." He pulled a pair of gloves out of his back pocket.

"Oh. Right. I told him I'd go over some of the procedures we discussed at dinner."

An odd stab of disappointment unsettled her. She'd actually gotten excited over the idea of having a patient to tend.

That was pathetic.

And Sam clearly wasn't himself. Did he regret last night? She hoped not. She wanted to kiss him and feel his arms around her. "Do you have time to sit with me and have some coffee?"

He stared at her as if she'd just spoken a different language. "I have chores to do."

"I know." She walked closer to him.

He purposely pulled on a glove. "I got a late start."

"Sam, we should talk."

"I reckon you want me to go back to the Golden Slipper," he said, studying the fit of the glove.

She stopped, totally dumbstruck that she'd barely given a thought to what should be done about getting home. Yet that's exactly what she should have been doing since she opened her eyes this morning—figuring a way to get into the Golden Slipper undetected. If Margaret was a Winslow, as revolting as the idea was, the answer undoubtedly had to be there in the brothel.

"*I* need to go to the Golden Slipper."

Sam's face darkened. "No."

"I have no choice."

He angrily pulled on his other glove. "Reckon I can't stop you, but if the sheriff catches you, I can't help you, either."

She bit her lower lip. The problem was, he'd try. She knew it even if he claimed otherwise, and that could get him hurt. "What else can I do?"

"You could stay," he said, so quietly she almost didn't hear him.

And then she briefly doubted her own ears when he strolled to the corner under the loft steps where he kept his tools, and picked up a shovel and a bucket.

"That's not possible," she replied.

"You can work with Doc. He'll tell the sheriff the same story I did about you being an old friend of his."

"What about Margaret?" Reese clasped her hands tightly together and pressed them against her midsection. The question was obviously moot, but that he'd even considered the possibility of her staying inspired an inexplicable longing inside her.

Without looking at her, he shrugged a shoulder.

"Reckon she'd give up after a spell. Might be that the next stage will bring the whore she'd been expecting."

Reese frowned. She'd never get used to the casual use of the term *whore*. Not if she stayed for the next fifty years. The fleeting thought made her a little queasy. It meant nothing, but even if she'd be stupid enough to want to stay, she had too many responsibilities back home. She couldn't have a brighter future ahead of her if she'd designed it herself.

Only twenty-nine and she was already considered part of the medical elite. She'd studied and worked with leading physicians in every field. A month ago, after finishing her residency, she'd been asked to…

*Holy crap.*

She swallowed convulsively. The names of several prominent doctors swam through her head, two of whom had actually mentored her. Learned physicians so brilliant that they'd earned their places in medical textbooks for eternity. She'd voraciously studied their practices. She'd worshiped at their altar. They'd discovered cures, published a myriad of breakthrough findings and made it possible for students like herself to carry the torch into the next frontier of medicine.

If she proved worthy.

The words vibrated in her head.

What had she proved so far? That she was attractive, thanks to luck and good genes, but to no credit of her own. That she was well-spoken and polished, thanks to the pricey prep schools she'd attended. Sure, her grades and recommendations had been impeccable, yet she'd tied for second in her class. Other med school graduates were equally qualified, if not more.

How had she forgotten basic humility? How had she gotten so full of herself that she assumed she deserved a spot beside those remarkable men and women who'd put years in and gained experience in medicine? Because she was the famous Brad and Linea Winslow's daughter?

The idea sickened her. Shame burrowed deep into her heart and soul. She could barely keep her head up.

"Reese?" Sam had come to stand in front of her, his work-roughened palms running down her arms, worry drawing his brows together. "Are you all right?"

She hadn't seen or heard him move. "I'm fine."

With a gentle hand, he lifted her chin and looked deeply into her eyes. "You're pale."

The concern she saw in his gaze touched her. No one ever worried about her. Why would they? Everyone thought she had it all. Other than Ellie, who had ever wanted to slay dragons for her?

She forced a smile, and shrugged. Sam thought she was this great doctor who performed small miracles. She couldn't tell him she was a fraud. "I guess I miss home."

For a second, regret flickered in his eyes, and then his expression went flat. He lowered his hand, nodded. And resumed his work.

SAM FINISHED REPAIRING the wagon, satisfied that it was in good enough condition that he could start renting it out again. Occasionally, men brought their womenfolk on the stage, and when they did, Sam got a decent price for the one buggy and wagon he kept in the back. Good thing no one had come asking for them. He should've had the wagon finished three days ago. But since Reese had shown up, most of his chores had gone to hell.

He pulled off his gloves, got a cup of coffee and stood at the entrance of the livery, gazing toward Doc's office. She'd been gone all afternoon, which was helpful for him getting his work done. As far as Sam knew, Doc had stayed sober, and that alone was as good as a body could hope for. Though damned if Sam hadn't missed her.

The boom of distant thunder made him look up at the blue sky. It was still clear in town, but dark gray clouds bunched over the mountains. They needed the rain. Everybody but the miners would welcome a drenching. Sam just hoped his roof held up. He'd been meaning to get up there and fix it, but it seemed there was always something else that needed doing.

And if he was to be completely truthful, deep down, he was beginning to wonder if his time in Deadwood might be coming to an end. One way or the other a conclusion was drawing near, whether at the end of a noose or on a trail back down to New Mexico or Texas.

The steady increase in travelers that came through town had been making him uneasy. Doc and the success of the livery had kept him rooted this long. Maybe too long. Sam was getting soft. Letting his thinking run crazy. He hadn't wanted to hear talk of Reese leaving. As if he had anything to offer her.

*Hell.*

He drained his coffee, and cast another glance toward Doc's place. The sun would be down in two hours and he hadn't given a thought to making supper. That was another bad thing about having a woman around; he couldn't just eat beans out of a can when he wanted. Tomorrow he'd see if she could find her way around a stove.

"Howdy, Sam."

He jerked, caught off guard by the deputy's voice, his hand instinctively going for a gun he never wore anymore. He relaxed his arm and shifted position to face the short, slim man. It angered him to no end that he hadn't heard the deputy coming. More proof he was getting too damn soft.

"Didn't mean to sneak up on ya." Lester grinned, his small black eyes glinting with meanness before he turned and spit.

"What are you doing down this way?" Sam asked the question, though he already knew that the sheriff must have sent him to poke around. Ames didn't like Sam, despite the fact he had never given the lawman reason.

Lester used his shirtsleeve to wipe his mouth. Most days he was too lazy to mount a horse, much less walk this far on his own accord, which made a person wonder how the man had ended up so bowlegged. He liked to stick near the saloons, especially the Silver Nugget, and when there was trouble, Lester took on the men too drunk to aim. Everybody in town knew the coward was a back-shooter, but the story was that he and the sheriff had been friends since they were boys, so no one said a word against him.

"Still looking for that runaway whore." Lester strolled past him to have a glimpse inside the livery. His steely gaze swept the row of stalls. "I heard a woman's been fixing up some of the boys from the mines."

Sam shot a glance toward Doc's office. He hoped she had the good sense to look out before she crossed the street. But if Lester walked too far into the livery, she might not see him till it was too late. "What does she have to do with Margaret's whore?"

Lester stopped at the last stall, where Sam kept his horse. "Heard she was a looker. You wouldn't be hiding her, keeping her for yourself, would you, Sam?" He snorted at his own joke, the irritating sound spooking Diablo. The horse tossed his head and pushed his powerful body against the stall door. Lester jumped.

Sam smiled. "The whore or the lady doctor?"

The deputy gave him a sour look before jerking his head toward the back room. "What's in there?"

Sam slowly walked toward the stove, every muscle in his body tensed. Martha's clothes were stacked in the box, but was the box tucked away? And what about his bedroll. "It's where I sleep. You want coffee?"

"Got anything stronger?"

"Nope." He picked up the kettle, poured more brew into his cup and then lifted the kettle in Lester's direction.

"Nah." The deputy moved away from the room and closer to Sam. "Doc's lady friend still here?"

Sam shrugged.

"The sheriff said you told him she left, but the stage driver don't recall taking on a single lady passenger. Fact is, he don't recall bringing one, neither."

Sam calmly sipped his coffee. He should be standing at the entrance and keeping Lester out in the open, to warn Reese. If she showed up there'd be hard questions, and then the sheriff would eventually come calling. Sam hadn't used his gun in a while, but good thing he kept it oiled and clean. "You been to Doc's yet?"

"I don't like going there. All those tonics he keeps…" Lester tried to hide a shudder with a loud cough that startled the horses. "It smells bad in that office," he muttered, moving quickly toward the street.

Sam followed him, annoyed when Lester stopped at the entrance, loitering as if he was in no hurry to leave. "You and the sheriff's got plenty to do. Doesn't make any sense you're worried about one whore."

"Might as well be barkin' at a knot, you ask me." Lester shook his head. "It's Margaret…she's still yappin' about that one, and you know how Sheriff Ames feels about—" The deputy stopped shooting his mouth off and scowled at Sam. "You see a strange woman, you come tell me or the sheriff."

"I'll be sure to do that."

Lester lifted his hat off his head and slapped it against his thigh while giving a final look around. "Yep, keep hearin' what a pretty thing she is. If we find her, I have a mind to take a poke at her myself."

Sam clenched his left hand, itching to hammer it into the man's slimy face. His other hand nearly crushed the tin cup he was holding. It took all his might to stay where he was, to keep his mouth shut, to let the deputy amble toward town. The notion of Reese lying with any other man filled him with a powerful fury that shocked him down to his boots. He'd never felt that deep burning jealousy over a woman. He didn't like it.

Even when Lester disappeared into the crowd in front of the Silver Nugget, Sam still didn't move. His jaw ached from being clenched and his temper hung by a shred. If Reese talked about sneaking into the Golden Slipper again, he'd surely throttle her. He thought about her smooth golden skin and her pretty pink nipples. About the surprising ripple of muscle along her thighs as she'd wrapped them around his waist.

Something wet dampened the front of his Levi's. He looked down and saw the stream of coffee coming from the tilted cup, which he hastily righted.

Hell.

Even when the woman wasn't around she strained his patience. He glared at Doc's office door as if Reese herself was standing there. Right as rain, she'd end up bringing trouble, but God help him, he wanted her to stay.

He wanted *her.*

"I THOUGHT IT WAS GOING to rain today. Did you hear the thunder?" Reese asked over dinner, frustrated by Sam's stubborn silence since she'd returned from Doc's a couple of hours ago.

"Yep."

"Think it still might?"

"Yep."

"Too late for snow though, right?"

He nodded.

She groaned, and he looked blankly at her. "Is there a problem?" she asked.

His brows drew together. "Nope."

That did it. No more trying to start a conversation. She was tired, anyway. Doc had had only one patient, a young boy with a nasty cut from a wire fence, which had required a few stitches. But that was all. Mostly they'd spent the day rehashing their previous night's discussion of sterilization techniques, CPR and difficult births. He'd had dozens of questions and did a lot of writing in his black notebook, but he'd said nothing of Sam or Martha, and Reese hadn't asked.

The whole afternoon he'd had only two glasses of whiskey. His eyes had stayed relatively clear, although without the whiskey his hands had been shaky. But he hadn't needed help stitching the boy. In all, she'd been pleased, and had enjoyed the time they spent together.

While Sam checked the water he'd been heating, Reese gathered their dirty dinner dishes and the pot he'd used to make a stew. She'd surprised herself by eating two helpings of the savory beef and carrots, along with two biscuits. If she didn't get some exercise soon, she was going to balloon up like a Macy's Thanksgiving parade float.

Her gaze strayed to the seat of Sam's worn jeans, and her pulse quickened as she thought of the kind of exercise she'd be getting in the next few hours. Oh, he might be giving her the silent treatment for whatever reason, but she'd seen the heated looks he'd sent her when he hadn't thought she would notice. Even if he did try to resist a repeat of last night, it wouldn't take much to make him see things her way.

She smiled at the thought and hummed while she scraped the plates and then measured out some soap flakes. Eyeing her with curiosity, he silently filled the small washbasin with water for the dishes, and then went back to heating more. She was about to ask what he was doing when he picked up the trough he used as a tub and carried it to the back room.

That was enough to send her pulse skittering, and she couldn't seem to wash the dishes fast enough. She dried and put them away and then threw another log on the fire, while he made several trips with metal buckets of heated water. Using a rag so she wouldn't burn her hand, she grabbed a remaining bucket, struggling not to spill any water because it was so much heavier than it looked, and joined him in the back room.

His bedroll had disappeared and disappointment churned in her stomach, but she reminded herself that room was needed for the tub. Still, she scanned the corners and behind the cot, hoping he'd stowed the bedroll nearby. He'd been acting oddly all evening and she couldn't help but wonder if he really did regret last night.

He easily lifted the bucket from her hands and dumped the contents into the trough. The water level rose to the midpoint, still low enough for them to both get in and not overflow. The fit would be tight, probably not very comfortable at all, but she was willing to try.

She looked at Sam and found him staring at her.

He quickly picked up two empty buckets.

"Sam." She touched his arm, stopping him halfway to the door. "Did I do something wrong?"

"No." He sighed. "I better put more water on the fire."

"That's enough," she said, casting a glance at the tub, mostly to avoid his eyes when she added, "With any more water and the both of us in there, it might overflow."

"Reese." He briefly closed his eyes, his anguished expression a complete mystery.

She withdrew her hand. "I don't understand. I thought you—I'm sorry."

He dropped the buckets and gripped her upper arms, his fingers digging into her flesh. "I'm not the man you think I am. Do you understand that?" When all she did was gaze back into his stormy eyes, he loosened his grip and his thumbs moved in a caress. "But I am a man," he said his eyes going to her mouth. "Not unmoved by temptation."

That's all she needed to hear.

# 15

REESE REACHED FOR HIS belt buckle, but Sam pushed her hands aside. She jerked her head up, her heart leaping to her throat. He cupped her face and kissed her gently on the mouth, and then kissed each closed eyelid, the tip of her nose and finally her chin. She stood frozen, instantly turned on as he went for the spot behind her ear, lingering there, before taking her earlobe between his teeth. It took a few moments for her to realize that he was unbuttoning her blouse.

He pushed the front of it open, exposing her bare breasts. Her nipples had already tightened to buds and he slowly circled them with his palms. She drew in a shaky breath and hooked her fingers into his waistband. He didn't stop her this time when she toyed with the buckle. Or even when she freed his belt. He was too busy learning the shape of her breasts.

She wasn't complaining. The way he wrapped his possessive hands around her flesh sent a shiver of anticipation racing down her spine. She couldn't seem to unbutton his Levi's fast enough, and he took the hint and pulled off his shirt. He worked on the hooks at the waistband of her skirt while she shrugged out of the blouse. In her enthusiasm to rid him of his trousers she'd forgotten about his boots, and chuckling, he sank back onto the cot before they both ended up on the hard ground.

Caught by surprise, she stared at him. "I don't think I've heard you laugh before."

He pulled off one boot, his mouth twisting wryly.

Upset that she may have ruined the mood, she crouched down and helped pull off his other one. "I like the sound. I like it when you smile, too."

His unsnapped Levi's rode low on his lean hips and her gaze followed the arrow of hair that disappeared behind his partially open fly. She moistened her lips, her breath quickening, and he reached for her, drawing her to her feet and settling her between his thighs.

As she stood before him, he reached around and ran his hand down her bare back to the curve of her bottom, then touched the tip of his tongue to her nipple. She clutched his shoulders for balance as he laved and swirled his tongue over the crown before drawing her hotly into his mouth. Her skirt hung loosely on her hips, and with one tug he sent the billowing fabric to a pool at her feet.

Hugging her closer, he groaned and buried his face in her breasts. She combed her fingers through his silky dark hair, arching against him and then stiffening when he lowered his mouth to the underside of her breast. She sucked in a breath when he trailed kisses lower, down the edge of her ribs, stopping to nibble the skin near her navel.

He brought his head up, his eyes glassy as he banded his arms tightly around her. "You're so sweet," he whispered, "so good," as if he couldn't quite believe it was so.

"The water is getting cold." She moved back enough to grasp his hands, and then she pulled him to his feet.

Without another word, she tugged down his Levi's. He quickly got rid of the trousers while she removed her running shoes. The more she eyed the tub the less she believed they'd both fit inside. It was definitely going to be interesting.

Before she could give it another thought, he scooped her up in his arms. She covered her mouth to stifle the surprised shriek she'd almost let out, and he smiled as he gently lowered her into the water. She hadn't seen him drop any of the scented salts into the tub, but knew he'd done it because the pleasant fragrance drifted up to greet her. The water was still delightfully warm and she tilted her head back to soak her hair.

"Aren't you going to join me?" she asked when he turned away.

He poured something into his hand and then rubbed his palms together as he positioned himself behind her.

"What are you doing?" She gripped the sides of the tub and twisted around.

He bent over and kissed her shoulder. "Face straight ahead."

"Why?"

"Reese."

She guessed what he was up to, couldn't quite believe it, but happily did as he ordered. He cupped her head with his strong hands and gently massaged in the shampoo. She closed her eyes and sighed.

His hands stilled. "Am I doing it wrong?"

She bit her lower lip, enjoying his touch, knowing Sam had never done anything like this before. "Oh, no. You're doing great. That was definitely a happy sigh."

He continued the massage, sudsing and then rinsing, his hands tentative at times, making her smile. But when he slid his palms over her shoulders down to her chest, there was nothing uncertain about the way he cupped each breast. He took the soap and slid it down her belly and rubbed between her thighs. She squirmed, which only fueled his determination, and his fingers quickly found that sweet spot that drove her to the edge.

She squeezed her thighs together, wanting him to stop, wanting him to touch her forever. "Sam, join me."

He broke contact, and then came around to the side and slipped his hands under her arms and lifted her out of the water. She started to giggle and he caught the sound with his mouth, kissing her deeply as she slid down his aroused body. As soon as she could stand on her own, she dried herself off while he rolled out the bedroll.

With a tenderness that brought a lump to her throat, he laid her down, making sure she was cushioned before lowering himself to his knees. He spread her thighs and kissed a path from the inside of her knee, only to stop tauntingly at the mound of curls. When she shifted impatiently she felt his smile against her skin. He used two fingers this time to enter her.

Instinctively, she tensed. He soothed her with whispered endearments and featherlike kisses along her inner thigh. Then he spread her nether lips and teased her with the tip of his tongue. She arched her spine and shifted her hips to the side, but he stayed with her, flicking his tongue over her clit until she didn't think she could take any more. She grabbed at his hair, torn between pulling him closer and pushing him away.

"I want you inside me," she whispered fiercely.

He slowed his pace, lulling her into a false sense of control before finding that magic spot that ignited a wildfire throughout her body. She came so hard she thought she'd shatter into a thousand pieces. Before she could recover from the explosion, he was poised over her, his arousal thick and ready, his hands cupping her bottom before he buried himself in her.

A STRANGLED CRY of pure anguish shattered the night's silence. Reese sat up with a start. Momentarily disoriented, she peered into the darkness. Beside her, she felt Sam stir restlessly. He murmured a few words before releasing a horrible moan. Disturbed by the noise, the stabled horses whinnied.

"Sam. Wake up, Sam." She shook his shoulder. "It's okay. It's just a bad dream."

"No," he bellowed, and bolted upright.

She shrunk from him, afraid that in his dazed state he might strike her. "Sam…" Tentatively, she touched his arm. "It's Reese. You're fine."

He grabbed her hand and squeezed it so tightly she cried out. Immediately he let go of her, drawing his arm back as if he'd been seared by a hot skillet.

"It's okay. You startled me, that's all." She laid her hand on his, and he turned it over until their palms met.

"I'm sorry," he said, his voice hoarse and broken. "I didn't mean to hurt you."

She squeezed lightly to show him she was okay. "You must have had a nightmare." It was too dark. She wished she could see his face.

He didn't respond.

"Do you remember it?" she asked, and when he still didn't answer, she prompted, "The nightmare. Do you remember what it was about?"

He pulled his hand away and drew the back of his arm across his forehead. Heat radiated from him. Just like last night, when she'd heard him moaning and had pressed a cool cloth to the back of his neck. If it wasn't so dark, if she could see, she'd get another cool compress.

"I'm going to light the lantern," she stated.

"No." His hand shot out, restraining her.

"Okay." She settled back down, his tension almost a tangible thing between them. "Will you tell me about it?"

Sam sighed with disgust and angled his body away from her.

She snuggled close, looped her arms around his broad shoulders and pressed her breasts against his back. He tensed even more, but she'd expected that. His skin was feverish and clammy, and she made up her mind that she wouldn't allow him to push her away.

"Sam?"

"Go to sleep."

"No."

"Reese."

"Sam," she answered in a mocking voice.

He sighed again, slumping a little. "I don't want to talk."

"I know."

Silence stretched, and then he turned to her, his hands finding and kneading her breasts. He kissed her, forcefully, and she let him, but only for a few moments. And then she moved her head back and said, "Nice try. But I won't let you distract me."

He lowered his hands with an air of defeat. "Can't a man have some privacy?"

That stopped her. Although she wasn't going to get anywhere by playing fair. "Are you saying you want me to leave?"

"No." Her eyes had adjusted to the darkness and she saw him shake his head. "No."

She cupped his face in her hands. "Please, Sam. Talk to me."

He raked his fingers through his hair. "You don't want to hear it."

"I do."

"Trust me on this."

Frustrated, she shoved at him. "No, trust *me*." Emotion swelled in her chest. Her voice shook slightly. "I've been at your mercy for nearly a week. Granted, at first I had little choice but to depend on you, but it's different now. I made a decision to trust you. Can't I have some in return?"

He grabbed one of her wrists and brought her hand to his lips. "You'll hate me." He spoke in a voice so low she had to strain to hear him.

"I won't. I couldn't."

His laugh was harsh. "You will."

"Think you know me that well, huh?"

He shook his head from side to side, and then as casually as if he'd stated his intention to go make coffee, he said, "I'm a killer."

"You've mentioned that." Her voice caught. She cleared her throat and lifted her chin. "Tell me something new."

He snorted and looked away.

She knew he'd killed more than once. Had he been a hired killer? What had they called them...gunslingers? No, not Sam. "You must have had a good reason." Even though she wasn't about to let this go, she felt chilled suddenly and pulled the quilt up to her chest. "You know, to kill someone."

"Is there ever a good reason to commit murder?"

Reese gasped before she could stop herself. Murder and killing were two very different things. She didn't see Sam as a murderer. Or maybe she just didn't want to. She swallowed hard. "Tell me what happened."

"Why? Dead is dead," he responded flatly.

"I don't believe you murdered anyone."

He started to get up.

She clutched his arm. "Don't do this, Sam. I don't care about your past. I know the kind of man you are now."

"You don't know anything," he spat, the unfamiliar viciousness in his voice convincing her more than his words.

"Then tell me."

"Jesus." He shook away her hand.

"Help me to understand."

"Leave it be," he growled.

"I'll ask Doc."

Sam shifted toward her, so suddenly, she shrank back in fear. He jabbed a finger in the air. "You don't speak of this to Doc."

Good. Doc obviously hadn't told him she'd already asked about Sam's past. She tentatively laid a hand on his arm again. "Okay, that wasn't fair to threaten you. But you aren't being fair, either. You've shared nothing of yourself with me."

"Why would I? Because I bedded you?" The deliberate contempt in his tone found its mark.

She refused to wince, and lifted her chin a little higher. "Yes."

Sam sighed loudly. "Whores are simpler," he muttered.

"That's probably true. But I'm not a whore."

He looked down for a moment, and then brought his head up and stared at her. "You don't know what you're asking." He sounded less threatening, maybe even resigned.

"Oh, Sam." She risked touching him again, scooting closer and rubbing his cold arm. "Nothing you can say will make me think less of you," she promised, and prayed that was true. "Whatever wakes you in the middle of the night will just grow until it destroys you. Tell your story. Tell it again and again until it loses the power to hurt you."

She waited for him to process her little speech, and when he stayed silent she took a deep breath and said, "I'll go first. I'm about to tell you something that I should've told you before now, but I've been too much of a coward."

She paused, gathering her courage. "I saw a picture of you in a book a few minutes before I…" The whole idea of traveling through time still appalled her. She could barely utter the words. "Before I ended up here."

"A picture?" He sounded confused, and she could see enough of his features to know he was frowning. At least she had his attention.

"A photograph."

"I've never had my picture taken."

She swallowed. This was the hard part. "It was some kind of history book about Deadwood. Sam, I don't know how to say this." Fear and an overwhelming sadness washed over her. "It was a picture of you propped up in a coffin. You'd been hanged for stealing a horse."

He reared his head back. "Stealing a horse?"

She nodded.

"That's a damn lie. I'd never take another man's horse."

She smiled in spite of herself. He'd admit he was a killer, but stealing a horse, well, that was over the top. "According to the caption, it was Hastings Barnett's horse."

Sam stayed quiet for a long time, probably trying to make sense of what she'd told him. Finally, he asked, "Goliath?"

"Mr. Barnett's name was the only one mentioned. I assume it was Goliath."

Sam laughed, a bitter sound that stoked the growing sorrow in her heart. "After all I've done…hanged for stealing a horse," he murmured. "Well, like I said, dead is dead. That's more than I deserve."

The resignation in his voice infuriated her. Worse, it frightened her. "Why? You tell me why you think you deserve to die."

He hung his head again. "It's hard to explain to a woman. You don't understand the brutality of war."

She straightened. War? The Civil War? Had to be. Relief blossomed in her chest. Oh, why hadn't she paid attention in history class? "Sam, you're telling me you fought during the Civil War."

He pushed a hand through his hair but said nothing.

"You can't blame yourself for what you did as a soldier. War is horrible, but if you hadn't killed, you would've been killed. Yes, it's awful, but that's the way it is."

"It wasn't just about the war. We did things—" He shuddered and jerked away from her. "Evil things."

"Who's we? You and Doc?"

He nodded haltingly. "And Jake. All of Captain Quantrill's men. We never questioned him."

"You were soldiers. You did as you were ordered."

"We shot unarmed men."

She didn't pretend to understand the vagaries of war. "What side did you fight on?" she asked, curious suddenly.

"The Confederacy."

She hadn't expected that, but it was a different time, different morals, she reminded herself. "You fought for your beliefs."

His laugh was terse. "What I did had nothing to do with my beliefs. Captain Quantrill was willing to hire us on. That's all we cared about."

"Yes, but—" And then a sudden thought struck her. "When was the war?" she asked, and he looked at her sharply. "How long ago?"

"It ended in '65." He paused. "I deserted two years earlier."

"How old were you when you joined the army?"

"Thirteen."

"Thirteen?" she repeated. "You were a child. What did your parents—"

"I didn't know my ma. She died birthing me." He

shrugged. "Reckon my pa may still be alive, but I haven't seen him for years."

She ached for the little boy who had no place to go but to join a man's army. "You can't possibly blame yourself for something you did as a child."

"I wasn't a child." His rebuke brimmed with self-loathing. "I was fifteen when we attacked Lawrence, Kansas. In the dead of night. Those men we killed weren't soldiers. They had something Quantrill wanted and we went in and took it. We wore the uniform, but we were no better than murdering thieves."

She tried to keep her voice steady. "Did you kill anyone?"

"One man," he replied quietly, pain thick in his voice. "He was so torn up, half his leg gone, blood everywhere. He begged me to shoot him."

She blinked back tears. That act of mercy hardly made Sam a murderer, but he wasn't in the frame of mind to listen to reason. "Is that when you deserted?"

"Jake, Doc and I hightailed it out of there before sunup."

"Did Captain Quantrill know? He could've assumed you were dead. In fact, he sounds more like an outlaw than an officer."

"It wasn't just Quantrill we had to hide from. The James brothers and Archie Clement, the whole lot of them loyal to the captain, they would've gunned us down if they'd seen us running. They'd kill us today if they saw us."

"As in Frank and Jesse James?"

He tensed. "You know them?"

"Um, not personally. I've read about them in books." She reached for his hands, persisting when he retreated. She squeezed them tightly and said, "You were a boy. A lonely, scared child who needed to belong. Don't confuse that boy with the good man you've become. Sam, look at me."

He stared into the darkness, his body rigid. The shame and agony he felt was almost a physical thing between them.

"You're a good man, Sam," she whispered. "I wish you'd believe that."

It broke her heart because she knew her words had no effect.

# *16*

THE NEXT DAY Sam checked Diablo's leg. The horse still had a slight limp, but if Sam stayed off him, in a week he'd be fine. Reese had gone over to Doc's first thing in the morning. She'd kissed Sam, offered to make their supper and then hummed all the way out of the livery.

Sam still couldn't believe it. He'd confessed his most shameful secret, and she hadn't run screaming from the room. She'd cried a little, but not out of fear or disgust. She'd cried for the lonely, confused child he'd once been. His chest tightened just thinking about the way she'd wrapped her arms around him and told him to let go of the past. How she'd told him that she was proud of the man he'd become.

An unexpected surge of emotion clouded his vision. He blinked, and then grabbed the pitchfork and started up the steps to the hayloft. Could be Reese really was touched in the head. That would account for her reaction. He couldn't think of another explanation. Except if she had the same feelings as he had for her.

He shied away from that loony thought. She was pretty and smart and kind to Doc. She had perfect curves and soft skin, and stoked a fire in him that no other woman had ever come close to feeding. Naturally, Sam liked her. But that was all. He didn't have any more feeling for her than that.

He forked hay down from the loft with a force that riled the horses. Goliath whinnied loudly, tossing his head and prancing around his stall. He sure was a fine looking animal. Though Sam tried to put it aside, the idea that he would steal another man's horse still unsettled him.

Nah, when the time came to meet his maker, it would be because one of the James boys recognized him. Or any of Quantrill's old gang. As for Captain Quantrill himself, he was dead. Sam had read that the man had come to his end at the hands of the Union forces in Kentucky back in '65. He'd heard Archie Clement had been killed a year later in Missouri, but that was just rumor. And even if it was a fact, the Captain's men would gladly put a bullet between Sam's eyes. Doc's and Jake's, too.

Hell, Jake might have passed on already. He hadn't seen him for nearly five years now, and Jake didn't believe in lying low. He liked his cards almost as much as he liked his women. Moreover, it didn't matter to him that the old gang wasn't all he had to worry about. The government had declared Quantrill's men outlaws. If any of them were ever identified as such, they'd hang for sure.

Sam swallowed hard. For the first time in his sorry life, he didn't want to die. He didn't want to leave Reese behind. He wanted to wake up each day with her beside him. He wanted her to fall asleep in his arms each night.

He gulped in the cool spring air. Hell, he was as crazy as she was. Reese would never stay. She was a lady, used to fine things. More than anything, she wanted to go home. And fool that he was, he'd promised to help her find the way.

"HAVE YOU READ ALL of those books under the bed?" Reese asked, as she reached for the pot. She was getting used to Sam's coffee—he didn't make it quite as strong as he had in the beginning. Even if he had, though, she'd have to force down the brew so that she could keep awake. They'd gotten so little sleep in the past three nights. Not that she was complaining. She yawned and smiled.

"Yep. Some of them five times."

"You definitely need some new ones." She poured herself a cup and set the kettle back on the fire.

"Reckon I've been too busy to read." He slid an arm around her waist and pulled her against his chest.

Coffee sloshed over the rim of her cup. "Hey." Laughing, she wiggled free. "Three days ago you were yelling at me to stay out of sight. Now you're practically attacking me in public."

His smile faded, and he turned away and pulled on his gloves.

Her own happiness deflated. Other than Ellie, she couldn't think of another person who had the ability to affect her mood as Sam did. In a small way, she resented the power that gave him. Not that she could change a darn thing. She'd fallen for him. As irresponsible and impossible as the situation was, she'd done the unthinkable. "What's the matter, Sam?"

"The sheriff hasn't stopped looking for you. Yesterday while you were at Doc's he came by again. I don't know how much longer we can put him off."

"I thought you told his deputy I was a friend of Doc's."

"I did." He shrugged. "I reckon the only reason he hasn't poked around more is on account of the trouble they've been having at the saloon."

She wasn't quite sure what Sam was trying to say. She took a cautious sip of her coffee, her mind grasping. And then the truth dawned on her. With Sam's past, he couldn't afford to have attention called to himself. God, she didn't want to consider how much trouble she could bring down on him and Doc.

How selfish she'd been these past three days, seeking the warmth and comfort she'd found in Sam's arms each night and not giving a thought as to how her presence might threaten him. Even Doc was at risk. She'd spent a good part of her days with him, helping with patients, answering his questions and describing the advances of modern medicine.

Since she'd been too thickheaded to get it, Sam was delicately reminding her that she needed to move on. Something else occurred to her. She shook her head in disbelief. She'd done nothing more to figure out how to get home. Her thoughts had run in the direction of improving how Doc sterilized his instruments, to convincing him that bloodletting and purging were not only ineffective but dangerous.

Was she suffering from Stockholm syndrome? Although she wasn't a hostage and in no way Sam's captive, she had depended on him for everything from the food she ate to the roof over her head. He'd hidden her and kept her safe, and it was entirely possible that she had mentally attached to him and disconnected from her real life. It was a textbook case, really.

"Reese?" He took her cold hand, his brown eyes warm with concern. "What's wrong, sweetheart?"

"I know I—" She swallowed, fighting the urge to bawl her eyes out. "Just hold me, Sam." She melted against him, comforted by his strong arms tightening around her. No, she wasn't out of touch with reality. She understood that she had to leave, but she also knew that this thing she felt for him wasn't some psychobabble nonsense. Screw the textbooks. What she felt had everything to do with him being the kindest, most decent, honorable man she'd ever met, could ever hope to meet.

And soon she'd never see him again.

Sick panic tied her insides into a knot. If protecting him meant she had to go, then she wouldn't hesitate, even if she had to get on a stagecoach, penniless, and ride as far away from Deadwood as possible. And away from the Golden Slipper and any clue that might lead her back to the twenty-first century. But she knew also, with absolute clarity, that no matter what, she couldn't leave until Hastings Barnett was gone from Deadwood, and Sam was safe. A fairy with a magic wand could suddenly appear and show her the way home and she wouldn't budge. Not if she thought for one second that it meant Sam could hang.

SHE WAS SITTING BY the fire rereading *Moby Dick* when Sam returned from Arnold's General Store. Reese glanced up and smiled, and his heart swelled like it was fixin' to burst out of his chest, the same as it always did when she looked at him that way. The woman had been here only a little more than a week and his whole life had been turned inside out. She even had him buying her unmentionables for her.

"I could've been the sheriff," he said, frowning, not that it would do any good. He'd warned her a dozen times not to sit out in the open when he wasn't around.

Still smiling, she shook her head. "I recognize your footsteps." Then she lifted her face for his kiss.

He obliged her, his blood heating even though he knew she wasn't offering to go to the back room and lie with him. She touched him often, and stopped to kiss him at the damnedest times. For no reason at all. At first he hadn't known what to think. Now he liked it. Made him wonder if that was something married folks did.

"I hope this is right," he said gruffly, straightening and handing her the wrapped bundle.

"Thank you." She eagerly pulled the string loose and stared at the brown kid leather gloves that lay on top. "What's this?"

"Gloves."

She laughed. "I know that. But it wasn't on my list."

"So your hands won't get rough and callused."

Her lips parted, but no words came out, and the sadness that entered her eyes tore a hole in his gut. They both knew she wouldn't stay. No need saying it out loud.

He shrugged. "You can take the gloves with you when you leave. You'll need them."

She pressed her lips together and bowed her head. She stared at the stockings and undergarments that he'd bought for her, and then abruptly looked up with a smile tugging at her mouth. "You're going to be the talk of the town, buying things like these at the general store."

Heat climbed up his neck and into his face. He decided not to tell her that he'd paid one of the girls from the saloon to make the purchase. But he was saved from having to reveal his secret when Doc hurried into the livery. Except he didn't like the grim look on his friend's face.

"Got something for you to see, Sam." Doc came close enough that Sam smelled the whiskey on his breath. He thrust out a newspaper. "It's bad."

Sam scanned the headlines. He didn't see anything at first, and then his gaze went to the article halfway down the page. "Son of a bitch."

Reese rose to her feet. "What's wrong?"

Sam studied Doc's bloodshot eyes. A bottle of whiskey sounded mighty good about now. His gaze went back to the article. Lamar Watkins was running for territorial governor. The last time Sam had seen the low-down skunk, he'd just shot an unarmed man in the back. And that wasn't the worst of his sins.

"Sam? Doc? What the heck is going on?"

Sam looked up and locked gazes with Doc. "I told her," Sam said quietly.

Doc briefly closed his eyes, but not before Sam saw the flash of pain he understood too well. "All of it?"

"Enough."

Doc stared at the ground before turning to face Reese.

Her lips lifted in a sad smile and she slid an arm around the doctor. "Don't be so hard on yourself. It was wartime. You were a kid."

He shook his head. "Sam and Jake, they were kids. I was nineteen."

Reese sighed. "That's not very old. In my time, boys are still in school at nineteen."

Sam and Doc exchanged glances. That was hard to believe.

"It's true," she said. "People go to school until they're in their twenties. I'm twenty-nine and I just finished medical school a year ago. But the point is, you were a soldier following orders. When you saw that your leader was evil, you left. You did exactly what you were supposed to do."

"We should've stopped him," Sam insisted.

"The three of you? No one would blame you for running as fast as you could."

"We didn't run," Doc commented, his shoulders straightening. "Not right away."

"Doc saved that young boy," Sam said. "And his ma. The pa was dead and their house had burned down. We took them with us. The James boys had gone crazy and we didn't trust they wouldn't hurt 'em."

Reese glared at Sam. "You didn't mention that the other night."

Sam didn't know what had gotten her so riled. He'd confessed all his ill deeds.

"You did a great thing. That was very heroic." She shot Doc an accusing look. "Both of you are so willing to dwell on the bad and not the good. Don't do it. It'll eat you alive."

His fist tightening around the newspaper, Sam met Doc's eyes. This thing with Lamar Watkins was what would do them in. How could they keep their mouths shut about the greedy, murderous bastard? He was pure evil. He didn't deserve the people's trust or the power of political office.

Sam cleared his throat. "We have to stop Watkins, Doc."

"I know."

Reese took the paper from his hands. She quickly found and read the article, and then looked up with a question in her eyes.

"He was one of Captain Quantrill's lieutenants," Sam explained. "Not officially, so the army doesn't know his name, but he did plenty of Quantrill's dirty work. He was there in Lawrence, Kansas. Gave the order to shoot whether a man was armed or not."

"Most soldiers killed because they had to, but Watkins liked it. He was one brutal son of a bitch," Doc added, and glanced at Reese. "Pardon my language."

She frowned at the newspaper. "How could he get this far without anyone knowing who he is?"

"He was one sneaky devil. Smart, too." Doc snorted. "Showed up only when it was time for the robbing and killing. He didn't leave no witnesses behind. Reckon the only men who'd know him are the ones who rode with Quantrill."

Sam studied Reese's face, preparing himself for the moment she understood what Doc was saying. Soon enough her green eyes widened and her face paled. "You're considered outlaws. You can't say anything about being part of that gang. You can't."

Sam looked at Doc, who scrubbed at his worn face. They both knew they'd hang for sure. But could they add cowardly silence to their many sins? There was no choice.

"Sam." Reese clutched his arm. The fear in her eyes tore at him. "Please don't be foolish. There has to be a way to expose this man without you and Doc putting yourselves in danger." She waved the paper at him. "Write an anonymous letter to the editor. Let a reporter dig around." She looked again at the newspaper. "This man who wrote the article—" She gasped and stared at something on the page, her face turning deathly white. Her fingernails dug deep into his arm.

"Reese?" He touched her cheek.

She wouldn't take her gaze from the paper. Her lower lip quivered. She opened her mouth, but no words came out. She seemed to be having trouble breathing.

A cold wave of fear trickled down Sam's neck. "Doc."

Reese waved a hand. "It's the date," she told them raggedly, holding up the newspaper. "Look at the date."

Sam had trouble taking his eyes off her, but he forced himself to look where she pointed. It was the 23rd of April.

"The picture I told you about—this is the date you're supposed to steal Hastings Barnett's horse."

"Maybe you'd better lie down," Doc said, frowning at her.

"Sam, you have to promise me you won't leave the stables for the rest of the day." Reese dug her nails in deeper. "That you'll stay away from Goliath."

"You have to calm down," Doc told her, his confused gaze going to Sam. "How about we get you a sip of whiskey?"

Sam hadn't said anything to Doc about what she had told him. He gave his friend a slight shake of his head, and then slid his arms around Reese. "I'll stay right here."

"Promise me."

"I swear on my life."

A pitiful sob slipped from her lips. Her eyes were dark, darker than he'd ever seen them. "Swear on *my* life, Sam," she whispered.

His gut clenched, and he swallowed around the sudden lump in his throat. "I swear."

She sniffed, and slowly nodded. "We'll get through this day. We will."

Doc sighed heavily. He rubbed his eyes and shook his head. "Reckon I'll go visit the Silver Nugget. The drunks over there make a lot more sense than you folks."

Sam watched his friend amble out to the street in search of his whiskey. He had a good mind to follow him.

REESE PUT AWAY *Moby Dick.* She'd tried to pick up where she'd left off, but kept reading the same paragraph over and over again. It didn't matter that she hadn't let Sam out of her sight, or that he'd kept his word and stayed close. She still worried. Was it possible to change history? Did she have that power? Would keeping him in the stables be enough?

Her mind raced and her jittery insides were driving her nuts. She couldn't seem to stop the tremor in her hands or slow down her pulse no matter how many deep breaths she took or what soothing lie she told herself. Because what if this date meant something to her, as well? Was today the day she could go back to her own time?

The wedding dress, Grandma Lily's house, the picture of Sam, they'd all played a part that fateful day in the attic. Was today the day all the pieces of the puzzle would come together again? None of it made sense, really, but neither did being hurled through time.

Oddly, the thought of going back didn't excite her as it should. Of course she wanted to see Ellie again, and her parents. Plus she was scheduled to be on another health news panel next week. She frowned. Was it next week? Or next month? She didn't care, she admitted. In fact, the idea didn't appeal at all.

Would anything else in her career ever compare to the work she'd done here with Doc? The sudden thought startled her. It was silly. Modern research and technology offered limitless possibilities to tackle age-old ailments. She could do so much good in the next thirty or forty years. Here resources were limited. She'd taught Doc everything she could. The patching and mending she'd done barely qualified as practicing medicine.

All this crazy meandering. Proof of her tattered nerves. She gave herself a mental shake as she watched Sam carry water to the stalls. A minute later, a young blond boy came running into the livery before she could hide.

Fortunately, he didn't see her sitting by the stove. He stopped in front of Sam and bent over, planting his hands on his bony knees as he tried to catch his breath.

Sam gave her a warning look and moved between her and the child. "What can I do you for, Tommy?"

Still breathing hard, after a false start he said, "Mr. Barnett over at the hotel—" Tommy stopped to catch his breath again. "He gave me two bits to tell you to get his horse ready. Says he's leaving town in twenty minutes."

Reese cupped a silencing hand over her mouth. Barnett was leaving town. Sam would be safe.

So why couldn't she shake the awful feeling of dread?

## 17

As soon as Tommy left, Reese flew at Sam. He caught her and swung her around in the air. She laughed, verging on hysteria. She kissed his cheek, his nose, his forehead. He slowly lowered her and captured her mouth with his. After a few moments, she was the one who broke the kiss. She hadn't noticed she'd been crying until he wiped a tear with the pad of his thumb.

"He's leaving," he said quietly. "Don't fret anymore."

She sent up a silent prayer of thanks and swiped at her other moist cheek. "Maybe my being here changed everything. Put some kind of kink in history."

He smiled. "I'm gonna go make sure Goliath is watered and fed before I saddle him."

She nodded, not as relieved as she should be. Her own words hadn't done much to convince her that history had indeed changed. There was no reason for her doubt, unless she believed in premonitions, which admittedly, best described the dark cloud of doom that seemed to hang over them.

She pushed back her cuff and checked her watch. Ten more minutes and Hastings Barnett would pick up his horse and leave Deadwood. In ten hours the hand would strike midnight and the day would be gone forever.

So might her opportunity to return home.

Reese's chest tightened. Maybe that was the reason for the dread. How could she leave Sam? She'd never find a man like him again. Not in her world. She knew she shouldn't have made love with him, she thought, as she watched him work, her heart squeezing at the familiarity of his every move. God, had she been foolish enough to fall in love with him? How could she possibly feel this way about him after only one week?

Wrapping her arms around her waist, she watched him lead Goliath out of his stall and tether him to a post. Speaking in a low, soothing tone to the horse, he strapped on the saddle. Reese tried to swallow, but her mouth was too dry. A wave of nausea swept her. Her vision blurred and she blinked to clear it. She leaned against a pole, feeling a bit light-headed, feeling a little like...

Reese straightened, fear slicing through her like a dull knife, her heart hammering her breastbone. She couldn't be going back. Not now.

No. No. Her mouth couldn't seem to work, so she reached out to him.

He didn't look up, but kept talking to Goliath, petting his neck, as if he didn't know she was there.

*No!* She heard the word echo in her brain. But it didn't make it past her lips. Sam and the horse blurred.

She told herself this was only about nerves and lack of sleep, and tried to take a step toward him, but her feet felt too heavy to move. She had to stop this from happening. "Sam!"

He glanced at her, and she breathed with relief. He'd heard her. Thank God, he'd heard her. She was tired and overwrought, that's all. Once Barnett left, everything would be all right.

But then Sam walked briskly toward the front of the livery.

She pushed away from the pole, and saw a boy, maybe fourteen, fifteen, run past the stables, hollering for Doc.

She hurried out to the street, where Sam stood.

The frantic boy pounded on Doc's door, yelling for him.

"He's not there," Sam called out. "What's wrong?"

"It's my little sister. Pa pulled her out of the creek but she's not breathing." The boy, red-faced, with fists clenched, jumped off Doc's porch. "I gotta find him."

"I can help," Reese said. "How far away is she?"

Sam looked at her uncertainly. "She's a doctor," he told the boy, his gaze still on Reese. "You have a horse?"

"Rode him too hard." The boy's voice broke. "He's lame."

Reese prayed it wasn't too late. "Timing is important."

Sam hurried back into the livery and in seconds returned with Goliath. "Take him. He's ready and he's fast."

Her heart nearly exploded. "Sam—"

"Save the girl," he said, and gave her a swift kiss on the mouth.

The boy didn't hesitate. He swung onto Goliath, and Sam helped Reese up. She didn't have time to argue. Every second counted. She barely had time to slide her arms around the boy's thin waist before he kicked Goliath into a canter. The canter turned to a gallop as they raced down Main Street, heedless of pedestrians yelling curses in their wake. They'd nearly made it out of town when she heard someone yell "Horse thief!"

She knew who would be blamed. Sam owned the livery. He was responsible for Goliath. But if she turned around now, she'd likely be issuing an innocent girl her death warrant. Reese closed her eyes and prayed as she never had before.

Jane sputtered, coughed, her little body jerking as she opened her big blue eyes. She blinked at Reese and coughed again.

Reese smiled at her. "What's your name?"

"Jane."

"Baby…" Seth Johnson nearly knocked Reese over in his haste to get to the girl. "Thought we lost you." He picked up his daughter and hugged her to his chest.

If Reese had met the big scruffy man in a dark alley, she would've had a heart attack. His black shaggy hair and even shaggier beard barely concealed the hideous scar running down his left cheek. The backs of his hands were heavily scarred, too, and he smelled as if he hadn't bathed in a month. He hadn't liked it that Reese had shown up instead of Doc, and unfamiliar with the CPR technique, he'd almost backhanded her. His son had stopped him.

She scooted over far enough so that she could get to her feet. She was a bit shaky herself. Until the child sputtered, Reese thought she might have been too late. But the girl hadn't hesitated in giving her name, which was a good sign that there was no brain damage.

The brother, whose name escaped Reese, stood off to the side, his hands jammed into his pockets. He still looked terrified. But he'd have to snap out of it because Reese didn't think she remembered the route to town. They were close, less than five minutes away, but she didn't want to waste any more time.

"I'm going to need your help getting back to town," she told the boy. "It's important that I hurry."

Seth Johnson looked up. "I'm obliged to you, ma'am. Don't reckon I know what you did, but you saved my girl."

"She'll be fine. I promise." Reese backed toward Goliath. "But I have to get back. This horse doesn't belong to me."

Seth's bushy eyebrows drew together. "Son, you take care of Jane. I'll git the lady back."

The boy's eyes widened. "Pa, the sheriff ain't gonna like it if you go into—"

"Do as I say, boy," Seth bellowed, and even Reese jumped.

He helped her onto Goliath, and then got his horse. The boy's comment about the sheriff made her edgy. She didn't need to bring trouble with her, but decided not to say anything until the town was in sight.

They rode hard and within minutes she could see Deadwood. Seth was slightly ahead of her, kicking up too much dust, and she urged Goliath to speed up until she was abreast of him. She called out, and he turned his fierce frown on her.

"I'm okay, Mr. Johnson. You don't need to go any farther."

He shook his head. "Best I see you back. Takin' a horse that don't belong to you is a hangin' offense."

"But I'm bringing him back."

He ignored her and kept riding. Although she'd been a good rider once, it had been a while and she had to concentrate on what she was doing in order to handle the powerful gelding. Maybe it wasn't such a bad idea to have backup. No matter what the differences between Seth Johnson and the sheriff, no one could begrudge her using the horse to help the man's daughter.

They got to the edge of town opposite Sam's livery and Reese immediately noticed the commotion. People crowded the center of Main Street. Her heart plummeted. She couldn't see what was happening, but she knew. God help her, she knew.

Without sparing Mr. Johnson a glance, she dug in her heels and rode Goliath as fast as he would go. The crowd that had gathered outside the jail parted when they saw her bearing down on them. In the middle of everything stood Sam, his hands in the air, the barrel of a gun pressed to his back.

She almost plowed into three women huddled near the boardwalk, but reined in Goliath just in time. "He didn't steal the horse," she yelled, hiking her skirt up so she could jump down. The women gasped at the expanse of bare legs visible as she slid off the horse to the ground. "I took Goliath. Let him go."

The man with a gold star on his chest and holding the gun on Sam glared at her. "It's the whore. Somebody grab her."

Sam used his shoulder to block a man who lunged for her. "Get out of here, Reese. Go. Now."

The sheriff slammed the butt of his gun into the back of Sam's head. He staggered, but stayed on his feet.

"Stop it. He didn't do anything." She surged toward the lawman, but someone grabbed her arm. She tried to jerk away, and saw that it was Seth Johnson.

He let go but got between her and the sheriff, a rifle in one hand, the fingers of his now free hand slightly curled and hovering over a pistol in his holster. "I reckon you best let the lady speak."

"What the hell are you doing here, Johnson?" The sheriff kept his gun trained on Sam, his fearful black eyes shifting to the left as if checking for backup. He obviously didn't want to tangle with Seth. "I told you to stay clear of town."

"Just makin' sure the lady was safe. She brought the horse back. Don't see where any harm was done."

"She's a runaway whore. Her word don't mean nothing."

"The woman saved my daughter's life." Johnson's hand flexed over the butt of the pistol. "Reckon that means somethin' to me."

Reese saw Hastings Barnett standing off to the side, his thumbs tucked into his belt, his face creased in an angry frown. "Mr. Barnett, please, no one stole your horse," she declared. "A little girl was drowning and I needed to get to her quickly. I took Goliath. Sam had nothing to do with it."

"Shut up," the sheriff screamed, his face contorted with fury. "Shut up, you stinkin' no-good whore. Don't you worry, Mr. Barnett. You'll get your justice. This man will hang before sundown."

Mr. Barnett glanced at his pocket watch as if annoyed with the inconvenience.

"No." Reese wasn't sure if the word had caught in her throat or made it past her lips.

"What's going on here?" Doc pushed through the crowd, obviously drunk, bouncing from one man to the other.

Reese's heart sank. Doc had been doing so well, and now that Sam needed him...

"Hell, Sam, what are you doing out here in the middle of the day?" Doc's unfocused gaze seemed to scan the crowd. His eyes met Reese's, and he winked, before lurching into the sheriff, who stumbled backward. "Pardon me, Sheriff Ames."

"You goddamn drunk." The sheriff shoved Doc, who spun around and used the momentum to take down the lawman.

"Sam." Reese pleaded with her voice, her eyes, her heart.

He hesitated, and then ran toward her and Goliath.

Another man wearing a badge launched himself at them, and Seth Johnson threw a punch that sent the man slamming back against the railing. Johnson drew his pistol and cocked it. "Anyone else?"

A collective murmur rose from the crowd as they hastily moved back.

Sam climbed on the horse first and then pulled her up behind him. He paused to look at Johnson.

The big man grinned. "Just havin' me some fun."

Sam nodded his thanks, wheeled the horse around, and they rode. Behind them Reese heard Johnson strongly suggest that everyone stay right where they were. She held on tight, her cheek pressed against Sam's back, her heart beating so fast that she thought it might fly out of her chest.

A few minutes later, she twisted around, and already Deadwood was out of sight. Sam took the right fork in the road and they rode another five minutes before he stopped at a dry ravine obscured by a thicket of cottonwood trees.

She stared at him in disbelief. "What are you doing? We can't stop. The sheriff will catch up to us."

Sam smiled sadly. "You can't come with me."

"What?" Frantically, she looked over her shoulder. At least they were hidden. "We'll talk later. We have to hurry."

"I'm a wanted man now, Reese. You were right about what you saw in that book," he said grimly. "That sheriff obviously aims to hang me. Go back. Tell them I forced you to come with me. Doc will protect you."

"I'm not leaving you."

He crooked his arm and motioned with his head. She realized what he wanted her to do, and, her hands shaking, she gripped his arm as she climbed down. He swung off Goliath and tied the horse to a pine sapling before facing her, his fingers painfully gripping her upper arms.

"Reese, listen to me. I have no money. I can't put a roof over your head. You go back now, and you'll have a chance."

She swallowed. "A chance at what?" she asked aloud, but the question was one only she could answer. Could she go back to her comfortable designer life and never, without a stab in her heart, think about him again? "I'm not leaving you, Sam."

He briefly closed his eyes, shuttering off the raw pain she'd already glimpsed. "You don't understand how hard life on the run can be."

"No harder than it will be without you beside me every day," she said, feeling the truth of that deep in her soul.

"Once you leave, you'll never be able to go back to the Golden Slipper. Or go home…" He looked pale, shaken. Even when he'd resigned himself to the thought of hanging, he hadn't looked so deathly afraid. So defeated.

She framed his face with her hands. Understandably, he thought she was being impulsive. But she'd already been put to the test. Earlier, when she'd felt faint, when she'd been terrified that she was going back…that's when her decision had been made. She knew it now. "I've already thought about this," she said calmly, her gaze fixed on his. "I came here for a reason, Sam. But it wasn't to change history. This was about us. We belong together. Tell me you don't feel that way, too."

His gaze roamed her face. "I don't deserve you."

"Stop it, Sam Keegan. I mean it. I won't have you saying anything bad about the man I love." At his shocked look, she laughed and threw her arms around his neck.

He hugged her close for a minute, and then looked down at her with such tenderness her heart swelled. "I feel powerfully glad to be alive every time I'm near you," he said quietly. "I reckon that's love."

She laughed and blinked back tears. "I reckon you're right."

"I wish it weren't so, but it's gonna be a hard life, honey," he warned, brushing an escaped tear from her cheek. "Doc and me, we can't let Lamar Watkins fool all these people."

"I know." She smiled. "That's what makes you a good man."

# Epilogue

*Four months later*
*A town fifty miles from Deadwood*

REESE'S LAST PATIENT of the day was leaving her office when Doc walked in. He looked good, his eyes a clear blue and his complexion no longer pasty, younger even than when he'd last visited, two months ago. She knew he still struggled every day, but he'd done a remarkable job of staying sober.

"Nathan." She smiled and rushed to him, holding out her arms. "I'm so glad you made it."

He hugged her soundly, and she was glad to feel more meat on his bones. "I wouldn't miss being here today...Doc." He grinned. "They callin' you that yet?"

"The women mostly." She pulled off her apron, plucked the pins from the bun at her nape and finger-combed the unruly waves. She usually wore her hair secured when she saw patients. That wasn't a problem. Getting used to long skirts and petticoats was the challenge. "Have you seen Sam yet?"

"Haven't been to the livery. I took the stage this time."

"Ah." The stage stopped at the hotel two doors down. "He should be here at any moment. Unless he has cold feet."

Doc chuckled. "Not Sam. Never thought I'd see the day he'd be making puppy dog eyes at a woman."

Reese smiled. Like any little girl, for her wedding day, she'd dreamed of the beautiful white gown, all the flowers, a lavish party for friends and family. At one point she'd considered asking Doc to bring the wedding dress from Grandma Lily's attic. Only the stained sleeves had to be repaired. But Reese wouldn't risk the possibility that the dress could send her back to a life she no longer thought about or wanted.

She missed Ellie. Her parents, too, though not like she missed her sister. But she couldn't think about that right now. More than anything Ellie would want her to be happy, and Reese couldn't imagine herself being any happier than she was with Sam. Amazingly, she also liked being a small town doctor and saving lives that would've been lost had it not been for her knowledge of modern medicine.

She pushed back her cuff, checked her watch, and a second later the door opened. Sam had changed to a crisp white shirt and black trousers. She smiled. "Don't you look nice."

He made a face and adjusted his string tie. Then he saw Nathan and nodded at him. "Thanks for coming, Doc."

Doc grinned. "It's not every day a man gets hitched."

"That's a fact."

Reese laughed. "Don't sound so grim or I'll get the wrong idea. Come on, I have a surprise for you."

Sam frowned, but let her lead him out of the office. Doc followed them down the boardwalk to the huge elm tree behind the smokehouse where she'd agreed to meet Ezra Bean.

New to town, the photographer had stopped by Reese's office earlier and offered to take their wedding picture. He was an odd little man, young but with old eyes, and she had no idea how he knew about them getting married, but she was delighted with the idea of having a wedding photo to hang in the house Sam was in the process of building them.

As soon as Sam saw the camera and tripod, he froze.

She squeezed his hand and tugged him closer.

Reluctantly, he moved toward the smiling Mr. Bean, who quickly positioned them. Doc stood off to the side, a grin on his face wider than the Mississippi. He'd been a good friend, selling Sam's livery for a tidy profit and arranging for her practice here in town. The people had been hesitant to accept a woman doctor, but he'd stepped in and soothed their worries.

They had lucked out when the owner of the local livery had decided to move back to Missouri. Between building their house and boarding horses, Sam was a busy man. With him and Doc, Reese had composed a letter to the newspaper questioning Lamar Watkins' suitability for territorial governor. They hadn't heard anything yet, but the election was still a ways off.

Her only regret was not having Ellie here. As if he'd sensed her sudden melancholy, Sam tightened his arm around her and lowered his head.

"I love you," he whispered, and kissed her at the same time the flash went off.

\* \* \* \* \*

*For the exciting sequel, don't miss Ellie's story.*
*ONCE A GAMBLER by Carrie Hudson,*
*available next month from*
*Harlequin Blaze!*

*Celebrate 60 years of pure reading pleasure
with Harlequin®!*
*Silhouette® Romantic Suspense is celebrating
with the glamour-filled, adrenaline-charged series*
LOVE IN 60 SECONDS
*starting in April 2009.*
*Six stories that promise to bring the glitz of Las Vegas,
the danger of revenge, the mystery of a missing diamond,
family scandals and ripped-from-the-headlines intrigue.
Get your heart racing as love happens in sixty seconds!*

*Enjoy a sneak peek of*
USA TODAY *bestselling author Marie Ferrarella's*
*THE HEIRESS'S 2-WEEK AFFAIR*
*Available April 2009
from Silhouette® Romantic Suspense.*

Eight years ago Matt Shaffer had vanished out of Natalie Rothchild's life, leaving behind a one-line note tucked under a pillow that had grown cold: *I'm sorry, but this just isn't going to work.*

That was it. No explanation, no real indication of remorse. The note had been as clinical and compassionless as an eviction notice, which, in effect, it had been, Natalie thought as she navigated through the morning traffic. Matt had written the note to evict her from his life.

She'd spent the next two weeks crying, breaking down without warning as she walked down the street, or as she sat staring at a meal she couldn't bring herself to eat.

Candace, she remembered with a bittersweet pang, had tried to get her to go clubbing in order to get her to forget about Matt.

She'd turned her twin down, but she did get her act together. If Matt didn't think enough of their relationship to try to contact her, to try to make her understand why he'd changed so radically from lover to stranger, then to hell with him. He was dead to her, she resolved. And he'd remained that way.

Until twenty minutes ago.

The adrenaline in her veins kept mounting.

Natalie focused on her driving. Vegas in the daylight

wasn't nearly as alluring, as magical and glitzy as it was after dark. Like an aging woman best seen in soft lighting, Vegas's imperfections were all visible in the daylight. Natalie supposed that was why people like her sister didn't like to get up until noon. They lived for the night.

Except that Candace could no longer do that.

The thought brought a fresh, sharp ache with it.

"Damn it, Candy, what a waste," Natalie murmured under her breath.

She pulled up before the Janus casino. One of the three valets currently on duty came to life and made a beeline for her vehicle.

"Welcome to the Janus," the young attendant said cheerfully as he opened her door with a flourish.

"We'll see," she replied solemnly.

As he pulled away with her car, Natalie looked up at the casino's logo. Janus was the Roman god with two faces, one pointed toward the past, the other facing the future. It struck her as rather ironic, given what she was doing here, seeking out someone from her past in order to get answers so that the future could be settled.

The moment she entered the casino, the Vegas phenomena took hold. It was like stepping into a world where time did not matter or even make an appearance. There was only a sense of "now."

Because in Natalie's experience she'd discovered that bartenders knew the inner workings of any establishment they worked for better than anyone else, she made her way to the first bar she saw within the casino.

The bartender in attendance was a gregarious man in his early forties. He had a quick, sexy smile, which was probably one of the main reasons he'd been hired. His name tag identified him as Kevin.

Moving to her end of the bar, Kevin asked, "What'll it be, pretty lady?"

"Information." She saw a dubious look cross his brow. To counter that, she took out her badge. Granted she wasn't here in an official capacity, but Kevin didn't need to know that. "Were you on duty last night?"

Kevin began to wipe the gleaming black surface of the bar. "You mean during the gala?"

"Yes."

The smile gracing his lips was a satisfied one. Last night had obviously been profitable for him, she judged. "I caught an extra shift."

She took out Candace's photograph and carefully placed it on the bar. "Did you happen to see this woman there?"

The bartender glanced at the picture. Mild interest turned to recognition. "You mean Candace Rothchild? Yeah, she was here, loud and brassy as always. But not for long," he added, looking rather disappointed. There was always a circus when Candace was around, Natalie thought. "She and the boss had at it and then he had our head of security escort her out."

She latched onto the first part of his statement. "They argued? About what?"

He shook his head. "Couldn't tell you. Too far away for anything but body language," he confessed.

"And the head of security?" she asked.

"He got her to leave."

She leaned in over the bar. "Tell me about him."

"Don't know much," the bartender admitted. "Just that his name's Matt Shaffer. Boss flew him in from L.A., where he was head of security for Montgomery Enterprises."

There was no avoiding it, she thought darkly. She was going to have to talk to Matt. The thought left her cold. "Do you know where I can find him right now?"

Kevin glanced at his watch. "He should be in his office. On the second floor, toward the rear." He gave her the numbers of the rooms where the monitors that kept watch over the casino guests as they tried their luck against the house were located.

Taking out a twenty, she placed it on the bar. "Thanks for your help."

Kevin slipped the bill into his vest pocket. "Any time, lovely lady," he called after her. "Any time."

She debated going up the stairs, then decided on the elevator. The car that took her up to the second floor was empty. Natalie stepped out of the elevator, looked around to get her bearings and then walked toward the rear of the floor.

"Into the Valley of Death rode the six hundred," she silently recited, digging deep for a line from a poem by Tennyson. Wrapping her hand around a brass handle, she opened one of the glass doors and walked in.

The woman whose desk was closest to the door looked up. "You can't come in here. This is a restricted area."

Natalie already had her ID in her hand and held it up. "I'm looking for Matt Shaffer," she told the woman.

God, even saying his name made her mouth go dry. She was supposed to be over him, to have moved on with her life. What happened?

The woman began to answer her. "He's—"

"Right here."

The deep voice came from behind her. Natalie felt every single nerve ending go on tactical alert at the same moment that all the hairs at the back of her neck stood up. Eight years had passed, but she would have recognized his voice anywhere.

\* \* \* \* \*

*Why did Matt Shaffer leave heiress-turned-cop
Natalie Rothchild?
What does he know about the death
of Natalie's twin sister?
Come and meet these two reunited lovers and learn
the secrets of the Rothchild family in*
**THE HEIRESS'S 2-WEEK AFFAIR**
*by* USA TODAY *bestselling author
Marie Ferrarella.
The first book in Silhouette® Romantic Suspense's
wildly romantic new continuity,*
**LOVE IN 60 SECONDS!**
*Available April 2009.*

# CELEBRATE
# 60 YEARS
## OF PURE READING PLEASURE
## WITH **HARLEQUIN**®!

## Look for Silhouette®
## Romantic Suspense in April!

# *Love In 60 Seconds*

### Bright lights. Big city. Hearts in overdrive.

Silhouette® Romantic Suspense is celebrating Harlequin's 60th Anniversary with six stories that promise to bring readers the glitz of Las Vegas, the danger of revenge, the mystery of a missing diamond, and family scandals.

---

**Look for the first title, *The Heiress's 2-Week Affair*
by *USA TODAY* bestselling author
Marie Ferrarella, on sale in April!**

---

# REQUEST YOUR FREE BOOKS!

## 2 FREE NOVELS
## PLUS 2
## FREE GIFTS!

**HARLEQUIN®**

*Blaze*™

**Red-hot reads!**

---

**YES!** Please send me 2 FREE Harlequin® Blaze™ novels and my 2 FREE gifts (gifts are worth about $10). After receiving them, if I don't wish to receive any more books, I can return the shipping statement marked "cancel". If I don't cancel, I will receive 6 brand-new novels every month and be billed just $4.24 per book in the U.S. or $4.71 per book in Canada. Shipping and handling is just 25¢ per book. That's a savings of 15% or more off the cover price! I understand that accepting the 2 free books and gifts places me under no obligation to buy anything. I can always return a shipment and cancel at any time. Even if I never buy another book, the two free books and gifts are mine to keep forever.

151 HDN ERVA  351 HDN ERUX

| Name | (PLEASE PRINT) | |
|---|---|---|
| Address | | Apt. # |
| City | State/Prov. | Zip/Postal Code |

Signature (if under 18, a parent or guardian must sign)

### Mail to the **Harlequin Reader Service:**
**IN U.S.A.:** P.O. Box 1867, Buffalo, NY 14240-1867
**IN CANADA:** P.O. Box 609, Fort Erie, Ontario L2A 5X3

Not valid to current subscribers of Harlequin Blaze books.

**Want to try two free books from another line?**
**Call 1-800-873-8635 or visit www.morefreebooks.com.**

\* Terms and prices subject to change without notice. Prices do not include applicable taxes. N.Y. residents add applicable sales tax. Canadian residents will be charged applicable provincial taxes and GST. Offer not valid in Quebec. This offer is limited to one order per household. All orders subject to approval. Credit or debit balances in a customer's account(s) may be offset by any other outstanding balance owed by or to the customer. Please allow 4 to 6 weeks for delivery. Offer available while quantities last.

**Your Privacy:** Harlequin Books is committed to protecting your privacy. Our Privacy Policy is available online at www.eHarlequin.com or upon request from the Reader Service. From time to time we make our lists of customers available to reputable third parties who may have a product or service of interest to you. If you would prefer we not share your name and address, please check here. ☐

HB09R

# You're invited to join our Tell Harlequin Reader Panel!

By joining our new reader panel you will:

- Receive Harlequin® books—they are FREE and yours to keep with no obligation to purchase anything!
- Participate in fun online surveys
- Exchange opinions and ideas with women just like you
- Have a say in our new book ideas and help us publish the best in women's fiction

*In addition, you will have a chance to win great prizes and receive special gifts! See Web site for details. Some conditions apply. Space is limited.*

To join, visit us at

# www.TellHarlequin.com.

# COMING NEXT MONTH

## Available March 31, 2009

### #459 OUT OF CONTROL  Julie Miller
*From 0–60*

Detective Jack Riley is determined to uncover who's behind the movement of drugs through Dahlia Speedway. And he'll do whatever it takes to find out—even go undercover as a driver. But can he keep his hands off sexy mechanic Alex Morgan?

### #460 NAKED ATTRACTION  Jule McBride

Robby Robriquet's breathtaking looks and chiseled bod just can't be denied. But complications ensue for Ellie Lee and Robby when his dad wants Ellie's business skills for a sneaky scheme that jeopardizes their love all over again….

### #461 ONCE A GAMBLER  Carrie Hudson
*Stolen from Time, Bk. 2*

Riverboat gambler Jake Gannon's runnin', cheatin' ways may have come to an end when he aids the sweet Ellie Winslow in her search for her sister. Ellie claims she's been sent back in time, but Jake's bettin' he'll be able to convince her to stay!

### #462 COMING ON STRONG  Tawny Weber

*Paybacks can be hell.* That's what Belle Forsham finds out when she looks up former fiancé Mitch Carter. So she left him at the altar six years ago? But she needs his help now. What else can she do but show him what he's been missing?

### #463 THE RIGHT STUFF  Lori Wilde
*Uniformly Hot!*

Taylor Milton is researching her next planned fantasy adventure resort—Out of This World Lovemaking—featuring sexy air force high fliers. Volunteering for duty is Lieutenant Colonel Dr. Daniel Corben, who's ready and able to take the glam heiress to the moon and back!

### #464 SHE'S GOT IT BAD  Sarah Mayberry

Zoe Ford can't believe that Liam Masters has walked into her tattoo parlor. After all this time he's still an irresistible bad boy. But she's no longer sweet and innocent. And she has a score to settle with him. One that won't be paid until he's hot, bothered and begging for more.